Locked Down with the BODYGUARD

Jax KANE

WHERE DANGER
MEETS DESIRE

Contents

Danger in Neon

Maria Sinclair

The club lights pulsed like a heartbeat, splashing pink and violet shadows across the bodies grinding on the dance floor. I was the brightest thing in the room. My neon teal hair was teased almost to the ceiling, silver dress clinging to every curve like paint, heels so high I could barely feel my toes. But that was the point. Feel nothing. Just be seen. Be noticed. Find Mr. Tonight Gone Before Morning Light. If I had my way about it.

"Maria!" someone shouted behind me, but I didn't turn around. I was too busy tossing back another shot of something neon and probably illegal. What did I care? As long as the music buzzed inside my skull, smoothing out the rough edges, it was all good.

My phone buzzed in my tiny clutch. I ignored it. Whoever it was could wait. Tonight wasn't for them. It was for forgetting. Like every night.

I danced harder, hips swaying with a man I barely knew. Maybe he was hot. Maybe he wasn't. All I saw were the shadows and his eager hands. This was my kingdom. One-night reigns, no attachments, no promises. Just a string of nights stitched together with glitter and fast choices.

Another buzz. Then three in a row. I finally pulled the damn phone out, squinting against the blinding strobes to read the scrolling texts.

Mia: *Get home now.*

Mia: *Something's wrong.*

Mia: *I think someone was in the apartment.*

The buzz of intoxication cracked.

I bolted past the bar, shoving through bodies that smelled like sweat and desperation. The cold slapped me in the face as I burst into the alley, heels catching on the broken concrete. I stumbled, cursed, and kicked them off, grasping my clutch to my chest as I flagged a passing cab.

The cab ride was a blur of flashing lights and rising panic. I told myself Mia was just high, maybe watching too many crime or horror shows. Maybe some party going on in the complex with the usual drunks in the hall. But when we pulled up to the apartment building, the street was eerily quiet. No party noise. No music. Just the hum of a streetlamp flickering overhead.

I handed the driver a crumpled bill and ran barefoot up the stairs. The front door was slightly ajar.

"Mia?" I called, heart pounding.

No answer. Where was she?

I stepped inside. The apartment was dark, the hallway light barely reaching the living room. The tv wasn't even on. Something was off. The air felt thicker, charged, like the seconds before a lightning strike.

I crept toward the living room. That was when I saw the shadow move. A man. Broad, heavy. Dressed in dark clothing.

He turned. I shrieked. The man lunged, and I ran. My bare feet slapped on hardwood, heart thundering in my chest. I didn't look back. I didn't need to. I hit the stairwell, leaped down steps, nearly fell but caught the railing. Someone shouted behind me, boots echoing.

Then, a screech of tires. A black SUV barreled around the corner, stopping inches from the curb. The door flew open, and a voice barked, "Get in!"

I froze. Another man, this one in tactical black, loomed in the open doorway. His face was shadowed, but I caught the glint of green eyes and the hard set of his mouth.

"No," I said, backing away. "I don't know you."

He lunged forward and yanked me inside like I weighed nothing. The door slammed shut just as a gunshot cracked behind us. The SUV peeled off into the night.

I thrashed against him, punching his chest with useless fury.

"Let me out! Who the hell are you?"

He didn't even flinch. Just shoved me into the opposite seat, his eyes scanning the windows like a machine. I kicked at the door, tried to open it. Locked. My heart pounded in my ears. I was trapped in a moving tank with a stranger who manhandled me like luggage.

"You can't just kidnap me!"

"You're welcome," he said flatly.

"What?"

He looked at me then. Really looked. Like he was memorizing every feature for a mugshot. His jaw was dark with stubble, his expression unreadable. Intimidating. The kind of man who wouldn't blink at violence.

"You're not safe anywhere. The Ortega cartel wants you dead."

My stomach dropped. I tried to laugh, but the sound came out thin and wrong.

"A cartel?" I repeated. "You're serious?"

"Dead serious." He didn't even glance at me. "Your apartment was compromised. Your friend's missing. And you were the next target."

"Mia?" I whispered. My throat closed around her name.

He nodded. "Gone when I arrived. Signs of a struggle. You were next on their list."

I pressed my back into the seat, shaking. "Why would a cartel want me dead?"

"Family ties. You're related to someone important on their radar. You were the easiest to reach."

"Bullshit," I snapped, voice rising with panic. "I don't know anything. I'm a nobody."

His gaze cut to me, sharp as a blade. "That dress says otherwise."

I flushed with sudden shame. I looked like a joke. Neon hair, skin-tight dress, glitter on my eyelids. No armor. No dignity. Just a walking party girl, a sparkling target.

"What's your name?" I asked, trying to sound brave.

"Luke Turner."

"That supposed to mean something to me?"

"No. But it might save your life."

We hit the freeway, weaving between cars with practiced precision. Luke drove like someone who had done this before, fast, focused, unflinching. I clung to the seatbelt and tried to process the last ten minutes of my life.

"You're in shock," he said.

"No shit, sherlock."

"Keep your head down."

I ducked lower, still trembling. My mind raced with images, Mia laughing earlier that day, the man in our apartment, the weight of Luke's arm when he'd pulled me inside. I reached for my phone again, but he snatched it before I could unlock it and tossed it out the window.

"Hey!"

"They can trace it. You're dark now. No contact, no signals."

"My whole life was on that phone."

"Then your life needs a reboot."

I wanted to scream. I wanted to cry. I wanted to be back at the bar with bad music and worse decisions, not in a speeding SUV with a stranger telling me people wanted me dead. But part of me, some scared, aching part, believed him. Because nothing in his voice sounded like a lie. And there'd been a man instead of Mia in my home.

Luke took an exit ramp, guiding the SUV down a narrow side street behind a line of warehouses. The city lights faded, swallowed by fog and shadows. We parked near a rusted gate, and he cut the engine.

"We switch vehicles here," he said.

I didn't move. This was some bad movie. Not *my* life.

"You planning to drag me again?"

"If I have to."

"Try it. I bite."

His lips twitched, almost a smile, almost human, but it vanished just as fast. He stepped out and opened the back. A second vehicle waited just beyond the gate, silver and nondescript. He must have stashed it earlier.

I followed, shivering as my bare feet touched cold gravel. The confident party girl was gone. What was left was raw and shaking.

Luke opened the door for me but didn't help me in. He watched me like a puzzle he hadn't solved yet. I slid in, hugging myself. The new SUV smelled like dust and leather, but it wasn't a new car, just different. He got behind the wheel and started driving again.

I finally whispered, "Where are we going?"

"Somewhere they can't find you."

The silence between us stretched. I stared out the window, still trying to believe this wasn't some drug-fueled nightmare. My mind replayed every memory of Mia. Had I missed signs? Had she known more than she let on?

"What happens if they do find us?" I asked.

Luke didn't answer right away.

"I won't let them," he said finally.

That should have been comforting. But the way he said it, like a vow written in blood, made my skin prickle.

We stopped at a gas station just outside the city limits. Luke filled the tank, scanned the lot, and came back with water bottles and a hoodie. He tossed it into my lap.

"Put that on. You're a walking beacon."

I slid it over my head, drowning in it. It smelled like him, clean, sharp, masculine. I didn't want to like it, but I did.

"Why are you helping me?" I asked as we pulled back onto the road.

He stared straight ahead. "Because it's my job."

But something in his voice made me wonder if it was more than that. And who made it his job anyway? What moron would take a job against a cartel? I didn't understand any of this. It still seems totally cray-cray. I couldn't have anything to do with a cartel or anyone involved with one. My dad was a CEO of some company. WE hadn't talked in eons and mom disappeared when I was maybe ten. Uncle died long ago while vacaying in Mexico. Luke had picked up the wrong girl.

We stopped at an old farmhouse nestled in a patch of woods, I didn't recognize. Gravel crunched under the tires as we approached, headlights cutting through the trees. Luke parked and scanned the area before stepping out.

He unlocked the front door with a key hidden beneath the porch rail, then motioned me inside. It smelled like dust and cedar. A stone fireplace took up most of one wall. The furnishings were sparse, functional, nothing personal. A hideout. I stood in the center of the living room, arms wrapped around myself. My feet were dirty and sore, used to being in shoes. Luke checked every room with methodical precision before returning.

"Clear."

My God. The only time I'd heard anybody say that had been on a tv show. He walked to a cabinet, pulled out a med kit and a gun, setting both on the counter.

"Bathroom's down the hall. Try to sleep. We move again at dawn."

I stared at him, exhausted but wired. "And if I can't sleep?"

He met my eyes, voice like iron. "Then stay alive. That's the only thing that matters tonight."

He turned away. I didn't follow, only rolled my eyes.

Rules of Protection

Luke Turner

The mission sounded simple on paper: keep Maria Sinclair alive. In practice, it was a goddamn nightmare wrapped in glitter and bad decisions.

"She's a mess, Turner," Chief Daniels had said, dragging a hand over his buzzed scalp as he paced the Sierra Bravo war room. "Drinks too much, parties harder."

I stood at attention, jaw locked tight. The screen behind him flicked through images, security footage, cartel insignias scorched onto a wall, a body bag being zipped up. Maria's father. Killed alongside his personal bodyguard, both executed point-blank. At least it wasn't one of ours. Sierra Bravo Security had never lost a client-yet.

"She doesn't know about her old man," Daniels added. "She was estranged. Don't lead with it."

"Understood."

"You're not her babysitter. You're her shield. Her uncle's in witness protection; the Ortega cartel is trying to flush him out by targeting her. No screwups, Turner. No attachments. Just deliver the girl alive to WitSec."

Alive. Not intact. Not unharmed. Just breathing.

Daniels had looked me dead in the eye. "You hand her off, you clock out. No room for failure."

Now Maria Sinclair sat in the back of my SUV like a cat in a cage, coiled, glaring, gorgeous in the kind of reckless way that got men killed.

"This is kidnapping," she snapped, arms crossed tight over a leather minidress. Her hair was electric-blue today, still tangled from the club.

I had stuffed a bag full of random clothes and her bathroom stuff in the moments I'd had before the intruder came along. Now I wished I'd left it all given she was just as obvious.

"You can't just throw me into a car and expect me to say 'thank you.'"

"I'm not expecting gratitude," I said, eyes on the rearview mirror. "I'm expecting you to stay alive."

She rolled her eyes. "Spoken like a guy who charges by the hour."

I clenched my jaw. "Your life isn't a joke, Miss Sinclair."

"Neither is my freedom."

The glint in her eye wasn't just defiance. It was fear wrapped in bravado. She was rattled. She just didn't know how to admit it.

We turned off the freeway, tires humming against asphalt. I'd already rerouted us twice, switching cars at a secured garage. She didn't need to know how close she'd come to being taken. And she had no idea the extent the Ortega cartel would go to get their prey. I did and every time I looked at her, it sent another cold bolt down my spine because I was all that stood between her and certain death. I glanced in the mirror again. She caught me looking.

"What?" she barked. "Hoping I'll cry or beg or something?"

"No," I said evenly. "Hoping you'll shut up before I duct tape your mouth."

She blinked, then smirked. "Kinky."

God help me.

"You got a phone?" I asked, already knowing the answer.

She hesitated, then fished it from her boot. I held out my hand.

"Seriously?"

"Cartel's got trackers. That thing is a GPS beacon."

She glared, then slapped it into my palm. "You gonna smash it like in the movies?"

"No," I muttered, tossing it out the window. "I'll get you a burner."

"You're also not fun."

"Wasn't hired to be."

We drove in silence for a while, her arms crossed and chin jutted like she was waiting for me to apologize for existing. I didn't. I scanned the road. Watched for tails. Took back roads through industrial zones and abandoned lots.

"Where are we going?" she asked eventually.

"Safehouse."

"Define safe."

"Harder to kill you there."

Her breath caught. A flash of real fear passed through her eyes before she masked it again. I was determined to shock some fear into her. To get her to pay attention to me.

"Why me?" she asked softly. "Why do they want me?"

"Your uncle," I said. "He got involved in some things he shouldn't have. They're using you to get to him."

"He's dead. I haven't even spoken to him in years."

"Doesn't matter. Blood is leverage."

So, she didn't know he was in WitSec. Another wrinkle. Not my job to inform her. When she finally stopped asking questions, I let the silence settle in. It wasn't peace. It was habit.

Later, when she was dozing in the passenger seat, head leaned against the window, breathing even, I pulled off into an abandoned truck stop lot. Nothing around for miles but sagging signs and the ghost of a vending machine.

I stepped out, leaving the engine running. The cold air bit through my jacket, and I leaned against the driver's side, pulling out my phone. The lock screen lit up with a photo I couldn't bring myself to delete.

Dani, smiling in the sun, her blonde hair caught in the wind. Sam, only eight months old, in her arms, grinning like the world had never hurt him. That photo was two weeks before the accident.

I closed my eyes. You didn't get second chances in my world. You got regrets. Nightmares. And, if you were lucky, enough armor to keep the next round from shattering what was left. Clients came and went. Missions ran hot and bloody. But family? That was sacred. That was gone.

Memory recharged, I put the phone away and climbed back into the SUV. Maria was still asleep, quiet, for once. I drove on.

We reached the safehouse just before dawn, a squat, single-story cabin buried beneath thick pine trees on the outskirts of Topeka. Steel-reinforced doors. Hidden cameras. Bulletproof glass. I'd cleared it myself last week for another client who ended up skipping the program. Their loss, her temporary gain.

Maria stepped out slowly, wrapping her arms around herself. Her heels sank into the dirt. She looked like a misplaced club flyer that had fluttered into my war zone.

"Do you have any normal clothes?" I asked, unloading the go-bag from the back.

She narrowed her eyes. "Do you always insult the people you're paid to protect?"

"Only when they make themselves easy targets."

"Not everyone was born wearing combat boots, Turner."

She stormed inside, muttering something about misogyny and emotional constipation. I didn't correct her. Not because she was right but because I'd been called worse by people I actually liked. Inside, she poked around the layout like she was searching for hidden cameras or exit routes.

"There's no Wi-Fi," she groaned.

"No distractions," I replied.

"No alcohol? No weed?"

I gave her a look. She flopped onto the couch, arms flung wide like she'd been shot.

"This is hell," she muttered.

I let her have the dramatics. Let her sweat out the drugs and alcohol. It was better than her trying to sneak out. I took first watch by the window, watching the tree line. We'd had no trouble getting here. It was quiet. Maybe too quiet. Maria eventually curled into herself on the couch, half-covered in a thin blanket, shivering but too stubborn to ask for help. I tossed her a heavier one without a word. She caught it mid-flight, muttered a soft thanks I pretended not to hear. I stayed up. Watching. Listening.

My phone buzzed just after 3 a.m. Unmarked number. No name. Just a blank contact and a message that froze the breath in my lungs.

Hand her over, and you live.

That was it. Just a quiet promise.

No one should have this number. I scanned the trees, every shadow suddenly suspicious. My thumb hovered over the alert button I had programmed to ping Tucker and Chief. Instead, I locked the screen and stood.

"Get up," I said to Maria.

She stirred, hair tangled, mascara smudged but somehow still looking vulnerably adorable. I bit it back. She was a client and under fire.

"What now?" she whined.

"Drills." I said harshly, to cover my inappropriate thoughts.

She blinked. "It's the middle of the night."

"We don't get attacked when it's convenient."

Her mouth opened to argue but something in my face stopped her. We moved into position. Quiet. Efficient. Like fire was coming. Because I knew it was. Maria followed me through the routine I had outlined with a ton of attitude, but she did it. No more eye rolls. No sarcastic comments. Just fast footsteps and sharp glances. She was scared. Finally. I hoped it would help keep her alive.

"Down behind the kitchen island," I said. "Cover your head. Count to ten, then move to the hallway closet. Stay low."

She nodded. Not a party girl now. Not a defiant brat. Just a twenty-two-year-old with shadows in her eyes and no one left to trust. But me. I took the perimeter while she practiced. I set up trip wires. Reinforced the windows. Adjusted the motion sensors. That message kept playing in my head.

Hand her over, and you live.

I'd seen men break for less. Swap lives like currency. But I wasn't built that way. Not anymore. Seen too much. Lost more. This girl, loud, unpredictable, half-wild, she didn't deserve the hell storm about to rain down on her. And maybe I didn't deserve to feel this angry about it. This... protective. Not again. But it was clutching my chest like an unscreamed battle cry.

I watched her finish the drill, breathless but determined. Then she looked up at me, just looked. She was expecting me to know the answers now. One thing I did know. The cartel wasn't bluffing. They were coming. And this time, I wasn't sure I'd be enough.

Chaos, Lipstick, and Loaded Guns

Maria Sinclair

The safehouse was cute, in a murdery sort of way. Pinewood floors, mismatched furniture, a fireplace that probably hadn't seen a real fire since the Bush administration. The only thing missing was a floral print throw and maybe a shotgun taped under the coffee table.

Luke had locked himself in the back room, brooding or doing bodyguard stuff. Which was fine. Great even. I wasn't used to sharing space with someone who didn't at least pretend to like me.

The man had zero chill. No conversation, no expression, just muscle and eyes that tracked everything like a hawk with PTSD. Definitely high on the hot bod scale but a total nothing on the interaction one. I didn't believe for one second that someone was out to get me. Yeah, my dad had enemies. He always had enemies. But I was a footnote in that story. A spoiled, rich, semi-famous nuisance with too many followers and too few secrets. So, somebody broke into my apartment. Happened all the time in the neighborhood.

So, I did what I always do when the walls feel too close. I slipped out. It wasn't hard. Luke was distracted by a call, and the side window in the kitchen opened with a gentle nudge. I pulled on the hoodie, wiped off the bright red lipstick, and was out the door before he even noticed.

Freedom. Cold air kissed my skin, and for a second, I could breathe again. I walked down the winding gravel path, letting the crunch beneath my boots drown out the panic I refused to name. I wasn't going far. Just into town, maybe. A café. Somewhere with espresso, Irish whiskey and a phone.

But I never made it past the first turn.

The van came out of nowhere. Black. Windows tinted so dark I saw my own reflection before I saw the man inside. The side door flew open, and a man jumped out, moving fast and silent like a nightmare. I screamed. Kicked. My elbow connected with something soft. A stomach? A groin? But there was another set of hands. I twisted, clawed, bit, and they dragged me halfway toward the van.

Then the night split open with a voice I never expected to be glad to hear.

"Let her go!" Luke's shout echoed through the trees.

Then gunfire! The hands dropped me. I hit the ground hard, shoulder-first. Pain bloomed, white and sharp. I scrambled away, crawling on all fours as the men ducked back into the van and peeled off. Gravel sprayed. Taillights vanished.

Luke was there in a blink, crouched over me, checking my arms, my legs, my face.

"You okay?" His voice was rough, tight.

I nodded, trembling. "Yeah. I think so."

He didn't move. Luke stood there, one hand still on my arm like he didn't trust me not to evaporate, a gun in his hand. His jaw clenched so hard I thought his teeth might crack.

"What the hell were you thinking?" he asked.

"I just needed air," I said. "And coffee."

His eyes darkened. "You could have been taken. You almost were."

The way he said it hit me harder than the pavement had. I'd seen him stoic, sarcastic, stone-faced. But this? This was fear. Not for himself, for me.

"I didn't know," I whispered.

He exhaled through his nose and looked away. "I didn't want to tell you like this."

"Tell me what?"

He was quiet for a long beat. Then, "Your father is dead. He and his bodyguard were executed. The same cartel that just tried to grab you."

The words didn't make sense at first. Like he'd said them in some other language. Then they landed.

My dad. Dead.

We weren't close. He was a ghost with a bank account and a name that opened doors I didn't want to walk through. But still. My heart lurched in my chest, and my fingers went numb.

"You think ... they're really coming for me?" I asked quietly.

"Don't you get it? They already are. They have." he said. "And they won't stop."

I didn't argue.

He helped me back to the house, one arm steady around my shoulders. I hated how much I leaned into him, how badly I wanted to feel safe again. Inside, he checked the locks twice, then pulled the blinds on every window. He moved like a man in enemy territory, and maybe he was. Maybe we both were. I sat on the couch, arms wrapped around myself, still shivering even though the room was warm.

"I didn't think it was real," I said in a little voice that didn't sound at all like me.

Luke didn't answer. He crouched in front of the fireplace and got a fire going with practiced efficiency. Sparks flared, shadows danced. I watched him like some strange woman who had just seen death and was trying to memorize the face of her rescuer. It was me.

"I've never been scared like that," I admitted.

He glanced back at me, something soft flickering in those battle-hardened eyes. "Good. Fear keeps you alive."

"That supposed to be comforting?"

"It's the best I've got."

I laughed, shaky and too loud. It wasn't funny, but if I didn't laugh, I might cry and I never cried. He stood slowly and handed me the blanket. I didn't thank him. Didn't have to. He just nodded once, like he understood. Then he turned to the window, watching the night. I pulled the blanket tight, pressing my face into the fabric. It smelled like cedar and wool and faintly of Luke. Solid and real.

For a long time, neither of us said anything. The fire popped. The wind tapped branches against the siding. I thought of everything I didn't say to my father. Everything I might never say to Mia again, either. I remembered hands and a black van. My chest tightened.

"You won't let them take me," I said suddenly.

It wasn't a question.

Luke didn't turn around. "No."

There was steel in that single word. No hesitation. No doubt. I believed him.

"Why?" I asked.

Now he turned. "Because it's my job."

"That's not what I meant."

He looked at me for a long time, eyes unreadable, and didn't answer. But I saw the way his jaw softened. The way his shoulders dropped just a little. Maybe he didn't know why either. Maybe it scared him too.

We went to our separate rooms eventually, both pretending the air wasn't thick with things we hadn't said. I lay in the dark for hours, watching shadows crawl across the ceiling. I was thinking some about Luke's arm around my shoulders. It had felt warm and real and in that moment, comforting. So unlike the men for the night I'd find at a club. Luke was realer than any of them had ever been. Somehow more solid and he was dedicated to protecting me from the bad guys. My feelings towards him were scaring me because I never felt anything for anyone. Cardinal rule one. Learned that from dear old mom and dad. Love doesn't exist. Never depend on anyone.

Just as sleep started to pull me under, my phone buzzed. A single text message. From Mia.

Help me.

That was all it said. And it was enough to freeze the blood in my veins.

I bolted upright, the phone slipping in my damp hands. For a second, I thought I imagined it. But the screen glowed again. Mia's message was real. I read it a second time. A third. No location. No follow-up. Just those two words.

I stumbled out of bed, heart pounding, and pushed open my door. Luke was already there. He had a gun in one hand, shirtless, his eyes scanning the hallway like he expected an ambush.

"What happened?" he asked.

I held up my phone. "It's Mia. She's in trouble."

He took the phone, read the screen, and nodded. "Where is she?"

"I don't know. That's all she sent."

He muttered a curse under his breath and turned back, pulling on a shirt as he headed toward the living room. "Get dressed. We're not waiting around."

"Shouldn't we call someone?"

"We will. But first, we move. They tracked the burner."

I was still shaking as I changed into jeans and boots. Luke was already keyed up, loading his gear, hands moving fast but precise. I couldn't stop thinking of Mia's voice, laughing on our last call. Texting someone was in our apartment. Then missing. Now she was calling for help. Was this because of me?

Flirting with Danger

Luke Turner

M aria sat on the edge of the bed, pale and wide-eyed, the phone still clenched in her hand like it might vanish. I took it from her gently, rereading the message from Mia. Two words. No location. No follow-up. It smelled like a trap.

"Tell me everything," I said.

She looked up. "There's nothing else. That's all she sent."

I didn't believe that. Not yet. "When did you last talk to her?"

"We live together. She texted she thought someone was in the apartment yesterday before you showed up."

"And you didn't think to mention that earlier?"

Her shoulders rose. "I didn't think it mattered."

Of course she didn't. Because she still didn't believe this was real. Not until that van. Not until the hands on her arms, dragging her toward something she wouldn't have escaped.

I ran a hand down my face, forcing the adrenaline to settle. "Gears packed. We're moving soon. But first, we need to eat."

She stood, stubborn as ever, chin tilted high. "You don't get to order me around like I'm some rookie recruit."

I stepped closer. "You almost died last night. You don't get to act like this is a game."

That silenced her. For a second, anyway.

I led her to the kitchen, flicking on the low cabinet light. It bathed the room in warm shadows, catching the edge of her cheekbone, the worry in her eyes. She poured herself water with trembling fingers. I watched, arms crossed, trying to stay grounded. I had seen too many civilians unravel under pressure. But Maria? She was holding it together by the thinnest thread.

I spoke low, careful. "You did good out there. You kept your head at the van."

She blinked at me. "Is that supposed to be praise?"

"It's what kept you alive."

She took a sip, then leaned against the counter. "So, what now? The van follows us when we leave? Or the text leads us straight to them?"

I didn't answer right away. I was too busy watching the rise and fall of her chest, the way her wild hair curled against her collarbone, the smudge of mascara still clinging to her lashes.

"I'll keep you safe," I said finally.

Her eyes met mine. "Yeah? Even from you?"

The question hit harder than it should have. I closed the distance between us in two steps. Her breath caught. We were too close now. Far too close for reason. But I didn't step back. Neither did she. She tilted her chin, defiant and beautiful. The kind of woman who didn't just walk into danger, she challenged it to a duel. And I had the nerve to think I could keep my distance.

"Maria," I warned, but my voice was low and wrecked.

She didn't flinch. "You keep saying this is just a job. Meaning I'm just a client."

I nodded, jaw tight. "Because that's the truth."

"Then why are you looking at me like you want to kiss me?"

I had no answer. None that would matter. She stepped closer, until her body brushed against mine, heat pouring off her like wildfire. Her hands slid up my shirt, slow and deliberate. My breath hissed through my teeth.

"You want to," she said, voice husky. "So do it."

And I did. The kiss slammed into me like a breaking wave. No hesitation, no thought, just instinct. Her mouth was soft and hungry, tasting of salt and something sweeter. Her fingers curled around my arms, pulling me closer. My hands found her waist, her hips, her curves like a roadmap I'd already memorized.

The world narrowed. Just the two of us. Just her lips and her skin and the low gasp she gave when I lifted her onto the counter. She wrapped her legs around my waist like she'd done it before, like this was something inevitable. My hand slid up beneath her shirt, fingertips grazing warm, bare skin. Her nails scraped the back of my neck, and I was drowning in sensation.

But even as heat surged between us, a sliver of warning pulsed beneath the surface. The ghost of every woman I'd lost whispered in my ear. *Not again. Not this.*

Maria kissed like a woman who didn't know the meaning of caution, like she'd spent her whole life behind glass and was ready to shatter every rule. And I? I wanted to break through right along with her.

"Luke," she whispered, and it wrecked me.

I kissed her again, slower this time. Deeper. Like I could burn the taste of her into memory. But my past didn't let go that easy. I stopped. One hand cupped her jaw. The other anchored me to the counter as I pulled back, breathing hard.

"I can't," I said.

She blinked, lips parted. "Why?"

"Because I've buried too many people I cared about. And I can't lose someone else."

She stared at me for a long moment. "I never asked you to care."

And that hurt more than it should have. I did not do one-nighters. And she was a client on top of that.

I stepped back, putting distance between us. The cold air hit my skin like punishment. Maria slid off the counter without a word, tugging her hoodie straight and smoothing her hair like armor.

"I didn't mean for that to happen," I said.

She didn't look at me. "You kissed me."

"You kissed me first."

Her eyes snapped up, fierce and flashing. "You didn't stop me."

I opened my mouth, then shut it again. She was right. I didn't stop her. I didn't want to. The tension simmered between us, the kind that didn't just burn, it scarred. But it was nothing compared to the fear still sitting heavy in my gut. We were being hunted. And moments like this, as sweet and brutal as they were, could get us both killed.

"I need you to take this seriously," I said. "No more sneaking off. No more running your own play."

She folded her arms. "I get it."

"I'm not sure you do."

"I do now," she said quietly.

I looked at her then and saw the tremble in her shoulders, the shine in her eyes. She was scared. And stubborn. And beautiful. I believed she did get it. And she was too close to every edge I'd sworn never to fall over again. I was about to speak when the window shattered.

Glass exploded inward, a sharp report cracking through the room. I yanked Maria down behind the kitchen island just as the second bullet tore through the wall, sending splinters flying. She gasped, clutching my arm.

"Stay down," I said, already reaching for my weapon.

My eyes swept the room, adrenaline roaring back to full burn. I edged up, just enough to see. Nothing but shadows beyond the broken window. But they were out there. Watching. Waiting.

Maria stayed low, hands over her head. Her breathing was shallow, fast.

"I don't have a clean line," I muttered.

"What do we do?" she asked.

"We move. Get to the SUV."

"They'll see us."

"Better than waiting here to be picked off."

She nodded. No argument, no hesitation. That alone earned my respect. I motioned for her to crawl ahead. We kept low, slipping through the hallway as the house groaned around us. Another shot cracked into the front door. Wood splintered. Maria flinched but kept going. By the time we reached the back mudroom, I could see headlights flickering beyond the trees. At least two vehicles. Probably more. This wasn't a warning. It was an assault. But if they wanted her, they were going to have to come through me.

I threw open the gear cabinet near the exit and grabbed the backup rifle. Loaded. Safety off. Maria was behind me, pale but composed. I handed her a flashlight, the heavy-duty kind that could double as a weapon.

"You remember what I told you about cover?" I asked.

She nodded.

"Good. You stay behind me. Don't argue."

She didn't.

We slipped out into the icy dark, boots crunching over pine needles and old snow. My eyes adjusted fast, tracking movement beyond the tree line. They weren't charging yet. Still testing the perimeter. Cowards. I crouched behind the wood pile, using it for cover. Maria stayed close, her fingers curling in my jacket. A figure moved near the barn, too fast for a civilian. Tactical gear. Rifle. Professional. They had training.

So, did I. I took the shot. The man dropped, silent and clean.

Maria jumped at the sound. "You hit him?"

"Yes."

She didn't ask how I could tell. She trusted me.

I scanned the trees again. Two more figures advancing. Coordinated sweep.

I looked at Maria. "When I say run, you run. You don't look back."

She met my eyes. "Not without you."

Damn it. I didn't have time to argue. Not anymore.

Escape Plan Alpha

Maria Sinclair

The first bullet missed us by inches. The second embedded in the frame of the back door as we slammed it shut behind us. My lungs burned as I followed Luke into the trees, stumbling over roots and frozen ground.

"Go!" he shouted, low and sharp, waving me ahead toward the gravel driveway.

I didn't ask questions. I just ran.

The SUV waited where we'd left it, half-frozen, pine needles stuck under the wipers. Luke yanked open the passenger door and shoved me inside, then darted to the driver's side and jumped in. The engine roared to life. Another shot rang out, cracking glass. I screamed as the passenger-side mirror shattered. Luke floored it.

The tires spun for a heartbeat before gripping, and then we were flying down the narrow drive, limbs slapping the windshield. My heart pounded against my ribs, and I couldn't stop shaking. Behind us, headlights bobbed through the trees. They were chasing us. Real men with real guns. This wasn't a bad dream. This wasn't some tabloid sex or drug scandal.

"Hold on," Luke growled.

We hit the road, fishtailing onto the blacktop as he spun the wheel. The back end swung wide before snapping straight. The city lights were still miles away. But at least we weren't dead. We careened down the hill, the SUV rattling over potholes and frost heaves. My hands clutched the dash so tightly they went numb. I risked a glance behind us. One set of headlights. Maybe two.

"They're gaining," I said.

Luke's jaw clenched. "Let them."

We hit the edge of a bend, and I braced as he cut hard into a hairpin turn. The tires squealed, gravel spraying. We didn't slow. Another few seconds and the second vehicle behind us missed the curve completely, crashing through the guardrail and vanishing into the deep culvert below.

"Oh my god."

Luke didn't flinch. "One down." he growled.

The lead vehicle still followed, closer now. I reached into the glove box, not knowing what I was looking for. My hand landed on a handful of road spikes.

"You need these?"

His eyes flicked down, then back to the road. "You know how to throw?"

"I was varsity softball."

He cracked a grin. "Then get ready."

I rolled down the window, wind slapping my face, and waited for the right second. When the headlights surged close enough to blind me, I leaned out and threw the spikes into the lane behind us. The sound of tires bursting was the best music I'd ever heard.

The SUV sped into the outskirts of town, weaving through sleepy intersections and dark storefronts. Luke took three turns in quick succession, doubling back twice before sliding into the shadows behind an abandoned auto repair shop. For a moment, we just breathed.

"You good?" he asked.

I nodded, still catching my breath. "I don't think I'll sleep again until I'm forty."

He exhaled a short, bitter laugh. "Welcome to the job."

He handed me a duffel bag from the back seat. "There's a change of clothes. Disguises. Burn the old stuff."

I unzipped it and stared. Jeans, a plain black hoodie, cheap glasses, and a wig. "You came prepared."

"I don't do maybes," he said. "You either vanish or you die."

I didn't argue. I pulled out the wig. Yuck. It was a mousy brown shade that made me look like a background extra in a crime show. I shoved it on over my dyed hair, then paused.

"This is ridiculous," I muttered. I reached into the water bottle stash and poured a full one over my head, scrubbing the cheap blue dye out into the gravel.

Luke watched me. "You don't have to—"

"I do," I said, washing away the last of the glitter and fake lashes. "I have to see me again."

When I looked up, Luke was staring at me. Really staring.

"What?" I asked.

He blinked and looked away. "Nothing."

It wasn't nothing. I saw it. That flicker in his expression. The sudden tension in his shoulders. Like seeing the real me without the armor made something shift. I didn't press. We didn't have time for that.

"Let's move," he said, voice low.

We ditched the SUV a few blocks over, wiping it down and parking it behind a shuttered diner. From there, we hoofed it. No phones, no

GPS. We walked side streets, alleys, cut through a dog park and a skate lot until we reached an underground garage.

Luke used a key fob I hadn't seen him carry to unlock a dusty black sedan.

"This yours?" I asked.

"Sierra Bravo keeps stashes in every nearby city."

"How do I get a membership?"

He didn't smile, but his mouth twitched. That was something.

We climbed in. The car smelled like leather and old coffee. He handed me a burner phone from the glove box. "Leave it off. Emergency use only. Off-grid from now on."

"Got it," I said, slipping it into my jacket. "So where are we going?"

"East," he said. "Then south. Disappear for a while."

And just like that, I left my old life behind.

I watched the city slip past in the rearview mirror. Neon signs blurred into streaks of pink and blue. A homeless man lit a cigarette on a park bench. Two teens argued on skateboards. The world kept moving like everything was normal. But it wasn't. Luke drove like he'd done it a thousand times, shoulders square, eyes scanning constantly. I could tell he was thinking four moves ahead.

"What happens to people like me?" I asked softly.

He didn't look over. "If we do this right? You stay alive."

"That's it?"

"That's everything."

I turned back to the window. "I used to think nothing could touch me. Like I was living in a bubble."

"You weren't wrong," he said. "Until now."

There was no judgment in his voice. Just fact.

I reached up and pulled the wig off. My real hair, damp and tangled, stuck to my cheeks. Luke glanced over, eyes lingering longer than they should have.

"You look... different."

"Terrible, right?"

"Real."

That word landed hard. It felt like the truth. Raw and uncomfortable. Appreciative.

We drove in silence for a while. I tried not to think about Mia. Or my dad. Or the version of myself I couldn't get back. Because the problem with being real was my past rearing its ugly head and refusing to stay buried. Then my phone buzzed. Not the emergency burner. My burner phone.

I froze. It should've been dead, buried in a dumpster back at the safehouse. I fished it out of the bottom of my backpack, where I must've shoved it in the chaos of leaving The screen flashed. One message. No words. Just a video file.

Luke saw my face and pulled over immediately. "What is it?"

I handed him the phone. He pressed play. The video started with static. Then it snapped into focus.

Mia. She was tied to a chair in a dim concrete room; her arms lashed behind her back. A gag covered her mouth. Her eyes were wide and terrified. A fresh bruise darkened her cheek. She was alive. Barely. The camera zoomed in slowly, deliberately. Her breathing quickened. She shook her head, like she knew we were watching, like she didn't want us to see her like this. Then a man stepped into frame. He didn't speak. Just stared into the lens and held up a photo. Me.

The message was clear. Me or Mia. My stomach flipped.

Luke turned off the hone and handed it back. "We need to go dark. Now."

I nodded, heart racing. "What if we can't find her in time?"

"We will," he said.

I wanted to believe him. But I had never been more afraid in my life.

Luke drove with one hand while the other tapped a coded message into the burner. I stared out the windshield, barely seeing the road ahead. All I could picture was Mia's eyes, round with fear, silently pleading.

"How did they get my number?" I asked.

"They have money and access," Luke said. "Your contact list was probably compromised weeks ago."

I swallowed. "So, they could be watching everything."

"They are," he said. "That's why we disappear. We give them nothing else to track."

We reached a motel on the edge of a town so small it barely had a name. Luke checked us in under fake IDs. The clerk didn't even look up from her soap opera.

The room smelled like bleach and despair. I dropped onto the bed while Luke swept for bugs.

"Clean," he said. "For now."

I went into the bathroom and stripped off the last remnants of glam Maria Sinclair, the gloss, the mascara, the jewelry. I scrubbed my face until it was red and raw. When I looked up, the girl in the mirror looked like a stranger. No glitter, no games. Just fear. I came out to find Luke watching the burner screen. A video had started again.

And this time, Mia was crying.

No Going Back

Luke Turner

The motel room was quiet, too quiet. Maria was in the bathroom again, probably trying to wash the fear off her skin. I stared at the burner phone, scrolling through encrypted contacts until I found the number I didn't want to call.

Mia's parents. It rang once. Twice. Then her mother answered.

"Hello?"

Her voice was tired, wrecked. Like she'd been crying for days and had nothing left.

"This is Luke Turner," I said. "I'm working with Sierra Bravo Security."

There was a pause. Then, "Do you know where my daughter is?"

I swallowed. "No. But we saw her. A live video feed sent to Maria's phone. She's alive. I sent the details to my company."

"Oh God." She started crying again. I could hear her husband in the background, demanding answers. I gave them what little I had. They asked questions I couldn't answer. When I hung up, I felt worse than before.

I sat on the edge of the bed, elbows on my knees, staring at the faded carpet. Guilt gnawed at the edges of my focus. Mia was taken on my watch. Maria was nearly next. And I was the one who was supposed to stop this. So far, I was failing.

I pulled out the second burner and dialed a different number. One I hadn't used in years.

"Turner," a voice answered. Gruff. Familiar. "Damn. Thought you were dead."

"Close enough."

A beat of silence. Then, "This about the girl?"

"I need intel. Cartel movement. Ortega branch, Colorado and Texas borders. You still got ears down south?"

"Some," Turner said. "But they're twitchy. You kicking the wrong hive?"

"I didn't kick it. I inherited it and they were already buzzing."

"You always had bad luck with women."

I didn't rise to the bait. "Can you get me anything?"

"I'll try. Give me a day."

I ended the call and tossed the phone on the bed. My head throbbed. I used to feel sure of things. Of missions. Of right and wrong. Now it was a blur. All I knew was Maria was my responsibility, and people around her were being hunted like animals.

I stared out the window. The sun was rising, streaking red across the sky. Red sky at morning - sailors take warning. Wonder if that applied to us Marines.

I had a bad feeling we were just getting started.

The bathroom door creaked open behind me. I turned to see Maria, fresh-faced, barefoot, wrapped in one of the motel's scratchy towels. My throat tightened for no good reason. Or maybe it was a half-nude woman without all the pretense of hair dye and glitter covering up her gorgeous blond hair and face.

"You okay?" she asked.

No. But I nodded because that was my job. "I spoke with Mia's parents."

She lowered her gaze. "They must hate me."

"They're scared. But they don't blame you."

"Doesn't mean I don't."

I stood and crossed the room, keeping my voice calm. "This isn't your fault. You didn't bring this to her."

Maria sat on the bed, folding her legs under her. "You ever get tired of being strong all the time?"

I blinked. "What?"

"You sit there like the world can't touch you, like none of this phases you. But it does, doesn't it?"

I didn't answer. Because the truth was ugly. The truth was that I'd lost people. Too many. And this, this mission, this woman, this fear, felt like a rerun I didn't want to watch again, let alone live.

She looked up at me, eyes too sharp. "You're scared."

I nodded once. "Yeah."

And we just sat there, the two of us in a crumbling motel, both pretending we had time.

I checked my gear again. Ammo. Phone batteries. Burner SIMs. While I worked, Maria dug through the laptop I'd gotten from Sierra Bravo. I let her, mostly because I didn't know what else to do. And because I was starting to realize she might be better at some of this than I was.

"You've been quiet," I said.

Maria didn't look up. "I'm reading intercepted messages from the cartel. The ones Sierra Bravo decrypted. They're scrambled, but I know Spanish slang."

"You speak Spanish?"

"My dad thought it was important."

I didn't say anything. I just let her keep going. At least having something to occupy her, kept her from spiraling into a panic loop. Her fingers moved fast across the keyboard, eyes locked in.

"There's a pattern," she said. "Mentions of movement, routes, and... this phrase."

She turned the screen toward me. A block of text, ugly and clipped, ran across the screen.

"What's that word?"

She highlighted it. "Proveedor. It means supplier. But it's connected to your name. And this."

She pointed to another string. "Sinclair."

My gut dropped.

"That's your last name."

"No duh."

She said it like it was a betrayal. Like her name itself was poison.

"I think someone's feeding them info from our side," she said.

I swore and paced the room. "You sure?"

"I don't know who, but some of this stuff? I think it's internal. It's stuff they shouldn't have."

Everything in me went cold. Sierra Bravo didn't leak electronically. Our man Connor was a tech genius and had everything locked up tight. Not unless someone inside let it happen.

"Can you trace it?" I asked.

"Maybe. If I have time."

"We don't have time," I said.

She nodded grimly. "Then we better make some."

I sat down beside her, my mind spinning. If they knew her name, if they were using it in messages, then this was deeper than a hit job. This was personal.

"Sinclair isn't just your name," I said slowly. "It's your father's too."

She nodded.

I looked her dead in the eye. "Did he have ties to the cartel?"

Maria flinched like I'd slapped her. "He was a bastard, but not that kind."

"Money talks. So does leverage. Maybe they used him. Maybe he helped them without knowing."

"I don't know," she whispered. "We barely spoke. Not unless it was about appearances or press."

I stood and began pacing. "If your last name is in their data, they want more than revenge. They want something else. Maybe access. Maybe legacy."

Maria rubbed her hands together. "I think I can get into the database deeper, but I need an hour."

"You've got thirty minutes."

She glanced up. "And if I don't find anything?"

"Then we run."

She exhaled, then got back to work.

I watched her. She was focused, biting her lower lip, attractive as hell. And for a second, I felt that gnawing question again. What if I wasn't enough to protect her? What if this time, I failed again? And didn't get a chance to fix it?

I texted Turner again, sending him the scrambled block Maria had found. He didn't reply right away. That alone told me things were worse than I wanted to admit.

The motel clock ticked past seven. Morning crept in slow, casting pale lines across the carpet. Maria hadn't looked up once.

I checked the window. Nothing. No cars. No movement. But the stillness didn't comfort me. Then the burner rang.

I answered. "Turner."

"That code you sent. You need to get out of there. Now."

My spine went rigid. "Talk."

"That phrasing? It's old-school. Stuff they used in southbound laundering ops. Backdoor channels. Corporate fronts."

"Connected to Sinclair?"

"Not just connected. Founded. Her dad's company was a pass-through for shell accounts."

My blood ran cold. "You sure?"

"I'm never wrong."

He hung up.

Maria was watching me now. Her hands hovered over the keys. "What is it?"

"They used your father's name to build a pipeline," I said. "He might've been part of it. Or a pawn. Either way, you're the legacy they want to erase. Or reclaim."

Maria didn't speak. Didn't blink.

Then she said, "I found something else."

She turned the laptop toward me. And there it was in one word. "Sinclair."

Clear as day. Embedded in red-highlighted code.

My breath caught as I stared at the screen. The word Sinclair wasn't just floating in some obscure corner of a message log. It was center frame. Top-level directive.

TARGET: SINCLAIR.

Maria whispered, "They don't just know who I am. I'm the mission."

I focused on her. Her shoulders were squared. Her lips pressed in a flat line. No panic. Just quiet realization.

"You're not running anymore," I said.

She nodded. "I want to know the truth."

Another video file pinged again on her burner. She opened it with trembling fingers. It was Mia again. This time, she was screaming through the gag. And the background wall was painted with a word in blood-red spray paint.

SINCLAIR.

Artifacts and Alibis

Maria Sinclair

The motel walls were mustard yellow, streaked with water stains and cigarette ghosts. The bed creaked if you looked at it too hard. Luke had barricaded the door with a chair and jammed a folded credit card into the lock. Nothing about this place said safe. Certainly Luke's pacing and constant staring out the curtains didn't give off the impression he thought we were secure.

And yet, it was the first time in days I could breathe without flinching. Luke had gone out to sweep the perimeter, or find more burner phones, or whatever survivalist thing he did when he needed space. I didn't ask. I needed space too. Not from him. From the noise in my head. So, I painted. It was my go-to for quieting the noise from my past.

There wasn't a canvas, but I'd found a paper bag under the sink and tore it into rectangles. I used the cheap motel toothbrush and a plastic fork as brushes. For paint, I had mixed crushed eyeshadow with water from the vending machine. It wasn't art school, but it worked.

I painted until my knuckles ached and my breath slowed. Wild, messy things. A cracked highway. My father's ring. Mia's eyes. Luke's silhouette with a red sky behind him. Each piece was a confession. Each stroke, a scream I didn't know how to say out loud. When Luke walked back in, I didn't stop. I couldn't.

He stood in the doorway, holding a bag of fast food and a six-pack of bottled water. He said nothing at first, just scanned the room with those wary green eyes. Then his gaze landed on my makeshift gallery spread across the floor.

"Is that eyeliner?" he asked.

I didn't look up, just nodded.

He dropped the bag on the table. "You always paint like someone's chasing you?"

"Only when they are."

Silence again. I hated how comfortable it had started to feel. The quiet between us. The awareness.

He crouched near the bed, looking at the mess without touching anything. "That one looks like a cufflink."

"My dad's." I didn't mean to admit it out loud.

I kept working, letting the soft scratches of cardboard and makeshift brushes fill the space. Luke sat with his back against the wall, elbows resting on his knees like he was trying not to sink too deep.

"You ever talk about it?" he asked.

I wiped a smudge with my sleeve. "About what?"

"Your family. What happened."

I paused. Not because I didn't know what to say. But because I did. And no one had ever asked before and yet Luke had driven right to the heart of it in a couple of days. He'd seen past the party girl and straight into my art to glimpse holes in my past.

"My mom had an affair with a guy from her yoga place when I was six," I said in a rush before the words were trapped in my throat. "My dad was sleeping with his secretary. They both found out and started screaming matches. Mainly about how I had ruined their marriage and who had to take me in the divorce. Dad ended up the loser, I guess. So, he shipped me off to boarding schools to not have to deal with any inconvenience I represented. Got me lots of sympathy not having anywhere to go for the holidays. So much for believing there's anything called love."

Luke didn't move.

"My uncle used to babysit me sometimes," I continued. "He was nicer, but he had his own demons. Friends with people who scared me, even back then. Tattoos, guns, laughter that didn't feel safe."

I looked down at my stained hands. "I learned to smile before I could spell. Learned to flirt before I knew what it meant. It wasn't about fun. It was survival. No one hurts the pretty, happy girl. Right?"

Luke's jaw tightened. I saw it in the way his throat worked.

"I partied because being sober meant feeling things," I said. "And feeling things meant remembering I was alone in this big crappy world. But, hey, somebody always wanted to come home with me; so, all good."

He said nothing. Just watched me like he wanted to fix something he couldn't understand.

I set down the brush. "Bet you didn't expect that from your spoiled little rich girl."

"No," he said quietly. "But I see you now, Maria."

That ruined me more than any insult or fake sympathy ever could. Because I think I wanted him to see me. And I didn't know what to do with that. We sat like that for a while. Him with his unreadable expression. Me with a damp paper towel smearing eyeliner across cardboard. The air between us buzzed with something I couldn't name. Or maybe didn't want to.

He finally stood, crossed the room, and set the fast-food bag beside me. "You need to eat."

I reached inside and pulled out a burger wrapped in foil. The smell alone made me realize how empty I felt.

"You always take care of people?" I asked.

"Only the ones trying not to fall apart."

I raised an eyebrow. "I'm fine."

"You're a fire in a glass box," he said. "One wrong move and you'll explode."

"That poetic Army guy talk?"

"I'm a Marine and it's just true."

I didn't know whether to punch him or kiss him for that.

We ate in silence. He stayed close, but not too close. Like he wanted to give me room, but not enough to run or to deny what I'd said or his words either.

"I meant what I said," he added after a long moment. "I see you."

That again. My pulse kicked up. I hated how much I wanted him to keep saying it. Because no one ever had. But when I looked up at him, really looked, I saw the same fear in his eyes that lived in mine. So, I said nothing. And neither did he.

Later, while he checked the locks and reloaded his sidearm for the fifth time, I gathered my paintings into a pile. Some were ruined from too much moisture. Others looked too raw to keep. I tossed them all in the trash.

Luke noticed. "You don't want to save them?"

"I already did," I said, tapping my temple.

He gave me a long look before turning back to the door. We were two feet apart but galaxies away.

I pulled on the hoodie, the drawstring worn and frayed, and curled into the creaky motel chair with a bottle of water pressed to my chest.

My body felt wrung out. My brain even worse. Maybe from putting emotion on paper or saying things out loud. Maybe from Luke's words. Luke sat on the edge of the bed, gun in hand, facing the door.

"I used to think safety was just about being at a loud club," I murmured.

He looked over.

"But now I think it's about people," I said. "Who you trust to sit with you in the dark."

His eyes softened. "That goes both ways."

We didn't speak again for a long while. We didn't have to. But when his phone vibrated on the nightstand, the spell cracked. He grabbed it, scrolled through a few texts, then handed it to me.

"Recognize anything?" he asked.

And I did. It was a still frame. A man with a shaved head, blurred by security footage, standing beside an unmarked truck in what looked like an alley somewhere in the southwest. He wore a long-sleeved flannel shirt, but the cuff had ridden up slightly.

Just enough to show a tattoo. Not a big one. Just three lines and a jagged shape. But I'd seen it before.

My voice came out thin. "That's the mark."

Luke tensed. "What mark?"

"My uncle's friends. The ones who came around when I was a kid. They wore it too. I remember one of them joking that it meant 'freedom through loyalty.' My uncle had it on his shoulder. He made a big deal about it one night when he was drunk."

Luke swore under his breath. "General cartel brand?"

"No. Some kind of inner circle."

He started pacing, muttering to himself. "That's a connection. Family. Legacy. If your uncle was in deeper than your dad..."

He didn't finish the sentence.

I stared at the image, unable to look away. That symbol was supposed to be buried in childhood memories. Now it was all real again.

Luke looked at me. "We need to find your uncle."

I shook my head slowly.

"My uncle's been dead for ten years."

Luke froze.

"What makes you say that?"

"They found his body in Mexico. Said it was a robbery gone wrong."

"Who identified him?"

"Dad."

He dragged a hand down his face. "You said the body was found in Mexico. But who brought it back?"

"No one. Dad had him cremated there. Said it was easier and safer besides."

"That doesn't sound safer. It sounds convenient."

The room spun slightly. I felt like the floor had shifted beneath me. "You think he lied or faked it?"

"I think if the cartel's still using this symbol, and one of their guys is wearing it now, he may not be as dead as your father said."

"But why would my dad lie?"

Luke looked straight at me. "Because he was involved. Or afraid. Or both."

I turned toward the pile of discarded paintings, suddenly wishing I hadn't thrown them away. There had been something comforting about making something with no rules. Now everything felt like a rule I had broken by being born into the Sinclair name.

Luke picked up the phone again, stared at the image, and zoomed in. The tattoo was clear. Familiar. And dangerous.

"I'll run it through facial recognition," he said. "If we're lucky, it will id someone who forgot to conceal it."

I nodded. But I already knew. Luck wasn't on our side. Not anymore.

Unmasking the Threat

Luke Turner

I hadn't slept.

Maria had finally passed out on top of the covers, hoodie tangled, hair damp from the motel's rusty shower. She looked peaceful. Safer than I felt.

I sat by the window, burner phone in one hand and the laptop in the other, chasing leads while adrenaline still made my skin hum. The tattoo she'd remembered haunted me. The jagged three-line symbol wasn't just a memory. It was a flag. Cartel inner circle. Elite. Blood in, no way out was a cartel motto.

I ran a public records scrape through backdoor access. I was supposed to keep this system for missions. Classified fieldwork. Not chasing ghosts through old death certificates. But Maria's uncle wasn't a ghost. He was a WitSec shadow we'd just started to see again. Then I found it. A federal case file from ten years ago. Sealed. DEA operation out of El Paso. The lead witness had been listed as "deceased" six months later in a cartel retaliation case. His name? Franklin Sinclair.

Maria's uncle. He wasn't just connected. He'd turned on them. And someone had covered it up.

I stared at the screen, stomach twisting. That explained the mark. It explained the rage. And it told me one more thing. Maria wasn't just hunted. She was bait.

The motel room creaked with every wind gust. I double-checked the window latches, then opened a file buried in my encrypted drive. I shouldn't have looked. But I did. Two photos. Sarah and Caleb. Sarah, with her untamable curls and too-bright laugh. Caleb, with gap teeth and chocolate on his chin, waving at the camera. I'd failed them. I hadn't been fast enough. Hadn't known the cartel warning signs when the ambush was coming. All I had now was a scar under my ribs and a picture. I closed the file before it swallowed me whole. It was before Sierra Bravo, before Dani and Sam. I had too many ghosts.

But when I looked over at Maria, sleeping fitfully against a pillow stained with dye and tears, I saw echoes of the same damn failure. People who trusted me, hoping I'd be enough to protect them. I wasn't sure I could do it again. Not if it meant losing more than my own blood. She stirred, rolling to her side, and I forced myself to look away. The attraction was getting harder to fight. It wasn't just physical. It was something deeper, something dangerous. That made it worse. Because the moment I wanted something again, I risked losing everything. The last time that happened, I buried my child. I would not bury anyone else.

The burner rang a few hours after sunrise. Unknown number. Scrambled ID. I answered without a word. The voice on the other end was low. Familiar. Coated in regret.

"You're not going to like this, Luke."

I stepped into the bathroom and closed the door behind me. "Who is this?"

A pause. "Colson. From Bravo HQ."

Colson. Logistics lead. No field experience, but solid. Or so I thought.

"What do you want?"

"I'm calling off the books. No encryption. No names."

"You already used mine."

Another pause. "They have Mia. And they want Maria."

I felt everything in me still. "Say that again."

"They'll trade. Mia for Maria. Clean exchange. Unharmed."

"Who the hell is 'they'?"

"You know who. Ortega. And someone inside wants to make sure Maria doesn't get too close to the truth."

My voice was ice. "Is that someone you?"

"No. But I work with him. And I'm scared, Luke. They've got eyes everywhere."

"Why are you calling me?"

"Because you're not supposed to make it to the next safehouse."

I stared at the cracked tile wall, bile rising. "You're warning me?"

"I'm telling you to disappear. Or choose who you save."

The line went dead. I crushed the phone in my hand. And didn't feel a thing.

Maria was already awake when I came out. She was sitting in the chair, her hoodie drawn up like armor, watching the door.

"You were gone too long," she said.

I didn't answer. Just walked to the window, peeked through the blinds. A gray sedan circled the block for a second time. It was gone now. Maybe just a neighbor. Or maybe not.

"You okay?" she asked.

"No," I said honestly.

That surprised her.

"I talked to someone at Sierra Bravo," I added.

She tensed. "What did they say?"

"They offered me a trade. You for Mia."

Silence.

Then she stood. "And you're telling me because...?"

"Because I'm not doing it."

She exhaled, some mixture of relief and fear I couldn't name. "What if they come for me anyway?"

"They will."

"Then why stay?"

I looked at her. And that was the moment. The one I'd been dodging. The line between protection and desire. It snapped taut between us.

"I'm not leaving you," I said.

Her eyes softened. "Even if it kills you?"

I didn't speak. I didn't need to. I think we both knew the answer. And it scared us both more than bullets ever could.

We moved fast. I packed the burner drives and stripped the room of prints. Maria cleared the bathroom, wiping every surface. We didn't speak. We just worked. By the time noon approached, we were in the car again. Heading nowhere. Because nowhere was the only safe place left.

Maria pulled her knees to her chest and stared out the window. "You ever wonder if your life is just a rerun of someone else's worst day?"

I glanced at her with a smirk. "Every damn minute."

She didn't smile. "I thought being rich would fix everything. Turns out, all it did was make the knives fancier."

I didn't know what to say to that. So, I didn't. It was a damned accurate perception.

An hour later, I pulled into a truck stop on the outskirts of Denver. We fueled up and took turns washing our faces in the bathroom. I used the moment alone to swap out phones again. That's when I got the second call. Unlisted number. This one scrambled even tighter.

I answered with a flat "Go."

A female voice replied. Crisp. Efficient.

"Luke Turner, you are being hunted. Not just by the cartel."

"Who is this?"

"I'm with the Bureau. The FBI. And I'm telling you now."

"Tell me what?"

She didn't pause.

"There's a warrant out for Maria Sinclair's arrest."

I stepped behind the gas station, phone to my ear, pulse pounding in my throat. "You're going to need to explain that *real* slow for a dumb jarhead."

"The Sinclair name is tied to international laundering accounts," the agent said. "Ten years of fraud. Offshore activity traced back to her father's holding company."

"She didn't run it. She was a kid."

"Doesn't matter. The accounts are still active. Some have her name on them. Funds are moving again."

"That doesn't make *her* a criminal."

"No. But it makes her useful. And if she goes missing, the Bureau will treat it as obstruction."

I gritted my teeth. "And you're telling me this why?"

"Because not everyone in the Bureau thinks she's guilty."

"Then clear her."

"Not my call. But if she gets brought in without you there, someone will make sure she doesn't walk out again."

I stepped away from the wall, watching Maria through the windshield. She was laughing softly at something on the radio, unaware her freedom had just become a time bomb.

"What's your name?" I asked.

"Doesn't matter. But you need to move. Fast."

The line went dead. I walked back to the car, slid behind the wheel, and stared straight ahead. Maria looked over.

"What now?" she asked, getting awfully good at reading me.

I put the car in gear.

"Now we vanish."

The sun was high by the time we hit the backroads. I took turns without signaling, used rural routes, avoided cameras. We passed boarded-up barns, half-dead gas pumps, and not much else. Maria didn't ask questions. Maybe she sensed I was past the edge.

Finally, she broke the silence. "Something happened."

I kept my hands steady on the wheel. "The Bureau's looking for you."

Her breath caught.

"As in the FBI?"

"They think you're tied to your father's laundering network. And because those accounts are still moving and he's dead, they think you have to be involved."

She shook her head slowly. "I haven't touched anything. I don't think anyway."

"I know. But they don't care. And if they find you, they'll use you as leverage or bury you."

She was quiet a long time. Then, "Do you believe me?"

I looked at her. And it hit me again, that strange ache that said I'd walk through fire for this woman. That I already was. I was running with a fugitive and already guilty of obstruction myself. I did not care.

"Yes," I said. "I do."

She closed her eyes and whispered, "Then we keep going."

The tires hummed on sun-cracked pavement. Every instinct screamed at me to protect her. But some part of me knew this wasn't just about saving Maria anymore.

It was about stopping everything coming for her. Even if I had to burn the world to do it. And by God, I would.

Betrayed by Blood

Maria Sinclair

We didn't talk for the first hundred miles. The roads turned to dust and the sky stretched out into a pale blue lie. I pressed my forehead against the passenger window, trying to convince myself that if I stared long enough, the truth would change. It didn't. My uncle was cartel. Or had been. Maybe still was, alive and cartel. And my father, my clean, polished, nothing-if-not-professional father, had covered it all up. Maybe worse. Luke didn't push. He drove like he was part machine, scanning every mirror, every turnoff, every car that came too close. I could feel the tension rolling off him like heat from asphalt.

I felt like I was going to vomit.

We reached the new motel a couple of hours after noon. It looked like a half-finished shed someone had forgotten about. Luke went in first, checked it top to bottom, then nodded me inside. I dropped my bag and sat on the edge of the bed like it might vanish beneath me. He set water on the table and knelt by his gear bag, avoiding my eyes. I couldn't take the silence anymore.

"So that's it? No big speech? No 'I told you so?'"

Luke looked up slowly.

"I don't blame you."

"Well maybe I do."

He didn't flinch.

"You want to hit something, hit me," he said. "Just don't turn this on yourself."

"I trusted my family." My voice cracked and I had to get up to pace. "I put Mia in danger because I was too busy pretending everything was fine. I threw parties and played dumb while the people I loved were being used. And now she's—"

I couldn't finish.

Luke stood slowly. "She's still alive."

"How do you know that?"

"I don't," he said. "But believing she's dead won't help us keep you alive or save her."

I covered my face with my hands, bile burning the back of my throat. "I thought I was smart. Slick. Untouchable. And now I'm the reason someone's being tortured in some warehouse. Or dead."

Luke walked to the nightstand, grabbed my phone off the charger.

"What are you—"

Before I could finish, he slammed it against the floor. The screen shattered. He stomped once, twice, until it shattered like a fragile champagne glass under his boot.

"Tracker's gone," he said.

I stared at the wreckage.

"That was our link to Mia."

"That was a weapon pointed at your head."

I sat down hard on the bed.

"You always this charming when someone's entire world implodes?"

He crossed his arms. "Only when I care."

That shut me up more than I wanted to admit. We sat in the stuffy room, the broken phone still in pieces between us.

"You care," I repeated. "Is that what this is?" I actually hoped he'd say 'yes'. I needed him.

Luke rubbed his jaw like he wanted to take the words back. "It's not supposed to be."

"Right. Because I'm a mission. A paycheck."

He looked at me then, and the silence stretched until it hurt.

"I lost people," he said. "My wife. My kid."

My throat tightened. "I didn't know."

"You weren't supposed to. I keep that locked away for a reason."

"What reason?"

"Because if I feel everything, I fall apart and I can't afford to do that."

We sat with that between us. His grief. My guilt. Damn, I understood that all too well. All the unspoken things swirled like dust in the stale motel air. I felt stupid, socially inadequate.

"I can't undo what my family did," I whispered. "But I can't be the reason people keep getting hurt."

Luke moved closer, sat across from me. "Then stop blaming yourself. Help me stop this."

I shook my head. "I'm scared."

"So am I."

He reached out, just enough that his fingers brushed mine. We stayed like that. Not kissing. Not touching beyond that. But it was more intimate than anything I'd ever known. And it scared me more than creepy men or the bullets ever could.

The motel AC kicked on, rattling like it was coughing up its last breath. I blinked hard and stood, needing movement, needing air. I grabbed one of the thin motel glasses and filled it at the tap. The water tasted like old copper. Luke leaned against the wall, arms crossed.

"So, what's the plan?" I asked.

"We wait till dark. Then move, closer to the freight line."

"Why not head west?"

"They'll expect west. You're LA's favorite exile. East keeps us unpredictable."

I sipped the water, staring into the grainy mirror. "Do you think my dad was involved? Really involved?"

Luke didn't answer immediately. "I think he knew more than he ever told you."

"Then he let me walk around blind."

"Or he thought shielding you was protecting you."

I let out a dry laugh. "Well, that worked out just great."

Luke pushed off the wall, walked toward me.

"You're not your family, Maria."

"Maybe not. But I've got their name. Their blood."

"You've got choices," he said. "And you've got me."

I stared at him, wanting to believe it, terrified to. Then someone pounded on the door. My breath froze in my chest. Three rapid knocks. Then two slower ones. Luke's eyes snapped to mine.

"Get down," he cried.

Gunfire ripped through the door.

The first bullet shattered the doorframe. Splinters flew. Luke grabbed me by the arm and yanked me to the floor just as the second round punched into the lamp beside the bed. He rolled, drew his weapon, and fired twice toward the door.

"Back wall!" he shouted, already moving.

I crawled beside the dresser, heart in my throat, body shaking so hard I thought my bones would rattle loose. Whoever was out there didn't wait. Another volley blasted through the window, shattering glass everywhere.

"Stay low!" Luke barked.

I covered my head, crawling toward the bathroom. Luke moved like a shadow, staying close, firing only when he had a clear shot. The door sagged off its hinges now, a black boot kicking through what was left. The man who stepped through wore body armor. Not cartel. Government issue. Luke saw it too.

"FBI!" the guy shouted. "Hands where I can see them!"

Luke didn't lower his gun. "You're early."

Another agent followed. Then another.

Luke dragged me behind the mattress, his voice low. "They're not just here for protection."

I nodded, dizzy. By the look in their eyes, these FBI weren't here to save us. They were here to take me. Luke must have known it too. He didn't move. His body blocked mine completely. The barrel of his weapon tracked every twitch at the door.

The lead agent raised his hands slowly. "We don't want trouble. We're here for Maria Sinclair."

Luke's jaw flexed. "She's not going anywhere without a warrant."

One of the others stepped forward, sidearm loose in his grip. "We have one. Signed this morning. Federal."

I could barely breathe. "Why now?"

"Because someone leaked your location," the agent said. "We intercepted cartel chatter. You've got less than five minutes before they get here."

Luke swore under his breath.

"So, you're not here to arrest me?" I asked.

"You're a material witness in an international investigation. The cartel will use you to break open the shell accounts. You won't be safe until you're in federal custody, and you can't be out free."

Luke lowered his weapon slightly. "Then why the hell come in shooting?"

The agent looked to the window. "We weren't the first ones here."

I followed his gaze. Black SUVs were pulling up. They had no markings.

Luke snapped back into motion, shouting "Everyone down!"

He grabbed the nightstand, flipped it for cover, and pulled me behind the bathroom wall. Outside, the cartel had arrived. And they weren't knocking.

Gunfire lit up the walls. Bullets tore through drywall, sprayed ceramic from the bathroom sink. The agents shouted orders, returning fire, but it was chaos. Controlled, practiced chaos but chaos all the same.

Luke dragged me to the tub, the only thing in the room that might stop a round. I curled into it, arms over my head, while he crouched low, bracing himself between the edge of the wall and the toilet tank. Water started leaking onto the floor from a crack in its side

"You still with me?" he asked, voice tight.

"Yes," I choked out.

"Good. You see a way out?"

I peeked through the side window. "Back lot. Dumpsters. Fence line to the left."

He nodded. "We move on three. When I say go, you run and don't stop. You hear me?"

I grabbed his wrist. "I'm not leaving you."

He looked at me, eyes dark, jaw set. "You don't get to make that call right now."

I held his gaze. "Neither do you."

I wasn't going out there by myself. That would be crazy. It was a battle front. And I was an unarmed civilian.

A grenade hit the front lot with a dull thunk. *Bang, Flash.* Everything turned white.

Luke covered me with a bunch of shots and then we were out the window. We ran, ears ringing, boots pounding against pavement as the motel burned behind us. The only thing louder than the gunfire was my heartbeat screaming one word - *run.*

On the Run

Luke Turner

I tossed Maria in the passenger seat of some van, hotwired the ignition, and peeled out, gravel spitting behind us. Maria slammed the door shut and braced against the dashboard as I took a sharp left.

"Were those real FBI?" she asked, voice tight.

"Hard to say. Could have been the Bureau. Could have been someone pretending to be. Wasn't taking the chance."

She let out a breath like she'd been punched. "You think they were cartel?"

"Second team looked definitely cartel, and they were trying to take out everyone."

We needed distance, fast. I kept the van below highway speed to avoid attention and cut through back roads, hugged the shoulder when I could. My eyes flicked to the rearview mirror every few seconds. So far, whoever they were had kept each other busy enough, I didn't see pursuit. We were lucky. Though we had lost all our gear.

After ten minutes of silence, she whispered, "You think they were after me, don't you?"

"Yeah," I said. "You were the only variable."

Her face crumpled for half a second, then she reached for me. Not to strike, not to argue, but to hold on. I didn't expect the kiss. I didn't expect her lips on mine while I was still steering. But it was raw, desperate, and real. I kissed her back. Fully. Finally.

And for a second, nothing else mattered.

The moment broke when a semi roared past us, and I jerked the wheel slightly to stay in our lane. Maria pulled back, cheeks flushed, eyes glassy.

"I shouldn't have done that," she said.

"You did though," I replied, keeping my focus ahead. "And I'm not sorry."

Her mouth opened like she might argue, but then she slumped in the seat and stared out the window. We rode in silence for a few minutes before she spoke again.

"What happened to you?" she asked. "Before this job. You said you'd lost people."

I gripped the wheel harder. I didn't want to talk, but I also didn't want to lie.

"Different job, mission, woman and her child. A woman I loved." My voice cracked before I caught it. "And then I lost it all."

Maria turned to me, slow. "Cartel?"

I nodded once. "Wrong mission. Wrong place. They made sure I never forgot."

She didn't press, just rested her hand gently on my thigh.

I didn't push it away. I kept driving. The highway thinned into dirt roads, then flattened into nothing but scrub and shadow. Miles from the nearest town, I finally eased off the gas and pulled into a deserted rest stop. I killed the engine. Maria didn't move. Her fingers curled around the hem of her shirt, nervous. I could tell she was still replaying what happened in that motel, in this van, in her own head.

"We should switch out of this vehicle soon," I said. "They might be tracking it."

She nodded. "Do we have anything they could trace?"

That got me thinking. I opened the glove compartment and found an old road map, a candy bar, and, taped to the inside of the dash, a small metal device. My gut tightened.

"Get out."

"What is it?"

"A bug."

Maria scrambled as I pulled it loose with a pocketknife. It was slick, modern, and blinking red.

"Damn it. They're tracking us."

I crushed it under my boot, but we both knew it was too late. We had company coming. I yanked open the back doors of the van. Cleaning supplies, uniforms, empty boxes. I grabbed a janitor jump-suit and stuffed it in a duffel bag with anything that might be useful, binoculars, zip ties, rags, gloves, a ball cap. Maria pulled off her hoodie and tied her hair up. We didn't speak. We were too busy thinking. Calculating. Surviving.

I handed her the cap. "Wear this."

She tugged it low over her face without question. We were back on the road thirty seconds later, bug destroyed, hearts pounding. I kept checking the rearview, but it was quiet. For now. She spoke first.

"Is this what you do? Run from shadows? Look over your shoulder forever?"

"I don't run," I said.

She tilted her head. "Then what do you call this?"

I glanced over. "This is survival."

She looked like she wanted to argue. Instead, she said softly, "You're good at it."

"I've had practice."

The tension simmered between us, neither boiling over nor fading. The storm was still coming. And we both knew it. We reached a crossroads. One way led north, the other toward an old state park I remembered from recon maps. I made the turn without consulting her.

"Are you always like this?" Maria asked.

"Like what?"

"In charge. Bossy. Stoic."

I shrugged. "You want a different version of me?"

"I want the one who kissed me like he meant it."

That shut me up. For a beat, the air crackled. I looked over at her.

"You scare me," she said quietly. "But not because I think you'll hurt me. Because I'm starting to feel safer with you than I ever did with my own family."

I didn't know how to answer that. So, I didn't. I just kept driving. The woods grew denser as we approached the state park turnoff. Trees crowded the road, branches scraping the sides of the van.

Then my phone buzzed. But I destroyed it. I slammed the brakes.

Maria gasped. "What?"

I reached beneath the dash and pulled out a second bug, biting back swear words. They were still on us. This one was harder to spot. Sleek. Embedded in a custom magnetic bracket wired to the van's electrical system. Whoever was tracking us wasn't just watching, they were invested. And well-funded.

Maria's voice was a whisper. "They put more than one on us?"

I nodded. "Looks like it. Must have wired every car in the parking lot."

"Then we've been burning daylight for nothing."

"Not nothing," I said. "We learned they can't pinpoint us in real time. We still have time."

I crushed the second bug and tossed the pieces into the woods. Maria paced by the van, jaw clenched.

"We can't just keep running."

"No," I said, "but we can buy enough time to plan the next move."

She stopped, watching me. "What if they're in law enforcement? What if the cartel paid someone off?"

"They did. I'm sure of it now."

Her breath hitched. "Then who do we trust?"

I opened the glove box, pulled out the road map, and circled a remote airstrip I used to land on during recon days.

"Right now? Only each other."

We ditched the van behind a burned-out service station half a mile off the county road. I popped the hood and yanked two cables just to be sure it wouldn't give away our last location. Maria trailed behind me with the duffel bag slung over her shoulder. Her legs moved on autopilot, but her eyes were sharp.

"You really think we can trust no one?"

I slowed down, watching her carefully. "I think the second we do, someone else gets killed."

That silenced her. We hiked up the hillside and reached a ridge that overlooked the park's western access trail. I scanned the tree line with the pair of compact binoculars from the van and spotted what I feared: fresh tire tracks in the mud below. Not ours. They were close.

I pulled Maria down beside me. "We're not alone."

She reached into the bag and pulled out one of the cleaning gloves, then flexed her fingers.

"Then it's time to stop hiding," she whispered.

I couldn't help it. I smiled.

The sound came low and sharp. Not a gunshot. A buzz.

I pulled the handheld scanner from my side pouch and flicked it on. The lights spiked red the second it neared the duffel bag.

"Don't move," I said.

Maria froze. "What now?"

I dug through the bag and found it, a third tracker, wedged into the seam of the jumpsuit I had grabbed.

"They're not following the van now," I muttered. "They're following us."

I crushed it against a rock, but I already knew.

The cartel was close. Too close.

Safe Haven, Fragile Hearts

Maria Sinclair

The sound of Luke smashing the last tracker echoed off the rocks. He didn't say a word, just ground the remains under his boot until they were nothing but metal shards. His jaw was clenched tight in anger. His eyes scanned the trees like he was still expecting something worse to appear. I didn't ask if he was okay. Neither of us was. But we were alive. And right now, that had to be enough.

We hiked for miles, silent, breathless, half-expecting bullets behind every gust of wind. My legs burned. My lungs ached. Still, I didn't stop. Not when I caught the glint of a faded metal roof through the trees.

The cabin looked like it hadn't been touched in a decade. Maybe two. Slumped at the edge of a clearing, windows boarded, door half-rotted, but still standing. Luke pried the lock with a crowbar from the duffel bag. Inside, it was musty and dark. But it was dry. And for the first time in days, I breathed.

Luke checked every room first, moving like a man born for this kind of caution. When he nodded, I eased onto an old couch with springs that groaned under my weight. I half-expected it to collapse. He sat a tiny solar lantern in the corner and laid out the supplies we had left: a half-empty water bottle, two granola bars, and a bag of trail mix. It wasn't enough, but it was something.

"Better than a body bag," he muttered.

I looked up with a smile. "Thanks for not letting that be where I ended up."

He didn't answer, just gave a tight nod.

I ran my hands through my hair, trying to comb out the sweat and dust. "I've never had to count on anyone before," I admitted. "Not really. I always made my own messes, and I got myself out of them."

Luke sank onto the floor across from me. "Maybe that's why you're still breathing."

"Is that supposed to be a compliment?"

"Sure. If it helps."

I laughed. And I wasn't even sure why.

The cabin creaked around us. Dust floated in the beams of light spilling through the cracks in the wood. We were not talking, but something hung in the air between us. A fragile silence. A truce.

Luke finally spoke. "I used to have a buddy. Deployment in Helmand. Tough as hell. Kept this lucky rabbit's foot on his vest."

I glanced over. His eyes weren't on me. They were far away.

"He died in front of me," he said. "And I didn't even know his real name. Just called him Tex for eight months."

I didn't know what to say. I've never watched anyone die. Luke hasn't really opened up before and I don't want to ruin it.

He shifted, back against the wall. "I stopped letting people in after that. Figured there was no point if I couldn't even save the ones I liked."

My chest ached for him. For the weight he carried like it's strapped to his ribs.

"I'm not asking you to save me," I said softly.

"I know," he said, "But I'm trying anyway."

We ate what little food we had without ceremony. My stomach growled louder than I'd like, but I savored every salty bite of trail mix like it was a gourmet meal.

Luke ripped the label off the water bottle and handed it to me first. "You need it more."

"Because I'm delicate?" I asked.

"Because you talk more."

I grinned and drank. He was trying. That was something. When he took a swig, I studied him. The lines around his eyes. The faded scar on his temple. The way his fingers twitched, like he was still gripping a rifle or missing it. I was wishing for him to be next to me, those lips against mine, but I supposed now was not a good time.

"You ever think about leaving all this behind?" I asked. "Starting over somewhere else?"

He shrugged. "Sometimes. Doesn't feel real though. Like I wasn't built for normal."

I nodded slowly. "I know the feeling."

We sat together in the quiet, surrounded by pine and wind and everything unspoken. I thought about kissing him again. I thought about what would happen if I did.

The sun dipped low outside, turning the sky gold and violet. Luke found a blanket in a storage chest and handed it to me.

"You take the couch," he said.

"What about you?"

"I'll keep watch."

"Sleep, soldier. I'll take a turn too."

His lips twitched, the closest thing to a smile I've seen for hours. "You giving me orders now?"

"Damn right."

We settled into a rhythm, both of us pretending this was something close to normal. He laid across the floor on an old rug, arms crossed behind his head, eyes on the ceiling. I was tucked into the couch, clutching the scratchy blanket.

After a long pause, I whispered, "Why me?"

Luke turned his head. "What do you mean?"

"Why take this job? Why go through all this?"

He was quiet for a long time.

Then he said, "Because you looked like someone worth protecting."

I closed my eyes and pretended the warmth in my chest wasn't dangerous. But it was. I drifted in and out of sleep. The wind howled outside, rustling through dry branches like whispers that never quite formed words. When I opened my eyes again, Luke was still awake.

"You're not sleeping," I said.

"Didn't plan to."

"You don't trust me?"

He lifted his head. "It's not you I don't trust."

"Fair."

I sat up and wrapped the blanket tighter around my shoulders. The cabin was freezing, but his eyes were warm. Warmer than I expected.

"Do you want me to stop flirting with you?" I asked. The words slipped out before I could think twice.

Luke's expression didn't change. "Do you want to stop?"

I didn't answer. The answer was a firm and resounding 'no' and I wanted to do a lot more than flirt.

He leaned up on one elbow, voice low. "I know this isn't the time. But when it is, when we're safe, you and I are going to finish what we started."

My breath caught. Heat spreading in my chest. And for once, I didn't run from it. I let it linger. The air in the cabin grew still. Every sound outside seemed louder. Crickets. Wind. A low creak like footsteps on soft earth. Luke sat up. Not fast. Quiet. Alert.

"What is it?" I whispered.

He raised one hand, palm flat, telling me to stay still. I obeyed. He crossed to the boarded window, careful not to disturb the floorboards. From his belt, he pulled a small mirror and angled it to peer through the gap. His whole body went tense.

"Someone's out there," he mouthed.

I felt my blood turn to ice.

Luke motioned for me to slide off the couch and crawl toward the corner. I did. My knees made no sound on the wood. My breath stayed trapped in my throat. He pulled out his sidearm and flicked the safety off. Through the boards, I caught a shadow. A shape too upright. Too slow. It was not a deer. It was a man. And he was watching us. My fingers dug into the wood as I braced myself, heart hammering so hard I felt it in my throat.

Luke's voice was barely audible. "He hasn't seen inside yet. Stay low."

"What if he does?"

"Then we make him regret it."

I didn't know whether that was meant to reassure me, but it did. A little. The shadow outside shifted. I heard the crunch of boots on leaves. Closer now. Luke crept toward the back door, gun in hand. He moved like water, silent and lethal. I pressed my hands over my mouth to keep from making a sound.

The footsteps stopped. A beat passed. Then another. A face at the windowpane.

Luke's back stiffened. I glanced up just in time to see the edge of a silhouette against the glass. A gloved hand. A scarred wrist. Luke raised the weapon. I held my breath. We didn't move. Not a single breath louder than a whisper. Luke shifted position slowly, silently, until he had a clean shot at the window. I stayed low, blood roaring in my ears.

The man outside didn't speak. Didn't shout. Just stood there, hand resting against the glass like he was waiting for an invitation. Luke signaled to me. Get ready.

I gripped the heavy flashlight like a weapon and nodded.

Then the man took a step back. Another. His boots crunched once. Twice. Then nothing. He had gone.

Luke waited five more seconds before exhaling. "Could be a scout. Testing us."

My throat was dry. "Cartel?"

He nodded grimly. "They found us."

A silence stretched between us.

Then Luke added, "But they don't know who they're dealing with."

I looked toward the window, expecting the shadow to return. It didn't. But deep in the trees, something moved. We were not alone.

Second Chances

Luke Turner

I circled wide through the trees, the cold air burning my lungs. Each step was measured. Quiet. Deadly. The prowler moved with the caution of someone trained. Not just some junkie or local hunter. He was looking at the cabin like he already knew who was inside. I flanked him from the left. He never heard me coming.

One clean strike, an elbow to the neck, and he dropped like deadweight. Not killed. Just unconscious. I patted him down. No ID, but the tattoo under his sleeve was clear. Cartel. I drug him thirty yards off the trail, zip tied his wrists and covered him with a tarp from the van stash. He would wake up sore, confused, and very alone. Of course, I relieved him of his gun, rifle and radio. They would prove to be very useful.

When I returned to the cabin, Maria was curled tight on the couch, flashlight still in her grip. Her eyes snapped to me when I shut the door. I studied her, taking in the sharp angles of her face, the way her hair fell across her shoulders. She was attractive, no doubt, but there was something more to her, a quiet strength that drew me in.

"You handled it?"

I nodded. "He won't be a problem."

She exhaled. That sound was relief and trust and something else. She was looking at me like I was more than just her protection. Like I was something she wanted.

My pulse didn't slow. It shifted. Sharpened. I didn't realize how close we'd gotten until her fingers brushed mine. Then she was kissing me.

The fire crackled, its warmth enveloping us like a blanket. I felt my muscles relax, the tension of the day slowly melting away. Maria's presence was comforting, a steady anchor in the chaos. I found myself drawn to her, not just physically, but emotionally. There was something about her, a resilience, a quiet determination, that resonated with me.

Maria and I sat side by side, our shoulders brushing occasionally, the silence between us easy and natural. I felt a strange sense of peace, as if the world outside had ceased to exist, leaving only the two of us in this small, forgotten place.

It was Maria who broke the silence, her voice low and husky. "We're stuck here for a while," she said, her gaze fixed on the fire.

I nodded, my heart pounding in my chest. The realization of our situation, stranded, isolated, alone together, sent a jolt of awareness through me. It settled lower, below my belt buckle. I turned to her, my eyes meeting hers, and in that moment, something shifted. The air between us crackled with unspoken tension, a current of desire that had been building since the moment we'd stepped into the cabin. Maria's eyes searched mine, her expression unreadable, but I saw the flicker of something there, a vulnerability she rarely showed. I reached out, my hand brushing hers. Her skin was cold, but I felt a spark of warmth at the contact.

"Maria," I whispered, my voice thick with emotion.

She turned to me fully, her eyes locking onto mine. I saw the question in her gaze, the hesitation, but also something else, a longing that mirrored my own. I leaned in, closing the distance between us, my lips brushing hers in a gentle kiss.

It was a tentative touch, a question asked and answered in the same breath. Maria's lips were soft, her response, immediate and eager. She pressed closer, her hands tangling in my hair, pulling me deeper into the kiss. The fire crackled behind us, its warmth a stark contrast to the cold air that still lingered in the cabin. I pulled back slightly, my breath coming in short gasps. Maria's eyes were dark, her expression intense.

"Luke," she murmured, her voice barely audible over the wind's increasing roar.

I smiled, a crooked, lopsided grin that felt foreign on my lips. "Yeah?" I replied, my voice rough with desire.

"We shouldn't," she said, her words a mere formality.

I knew she wanted this as much as I did. I cupped her face in my hands, my thumbs brushing her cheeks.

"I know." I countered, my voice firm. "But we're alive, Maria. And in this moment, that's all that matters."

She hesitated, her gaze searching mine, as if looking for a reason to disagree. But there was none. The world was forgotten, leaving only the two of us in this small, intimate space. Maria's resistance crumbled, her lips curving into a soft smile.

"You're impossible," she said, her voice laced with affection.

"And you're stubborn," I retorted, leaning in to kiss her again.

This time, there was no hesitation, no question. Our lips met with a hunger that had been building for hours, days. Maria's hands moved to my chest, her touch sending shivers down my spine. I pulled her closer, my arms wrapping around her, holding her tight against me.

The kiss deepened, our tongues tangling in a dance that was both familiar and new. I tasted her, the sweetness of her lips, the hint of mint on her breath, and felt a surge of desire that threatened to consume me. Maria's body pressed against mine, her curves fitting perfectly into the hollows of my own. I groaned, the sound muffled against her lips, as my hands moved to her waist, pulling her even closer.

We broke apart, both of us breathless, our hearts pounding in unison. Maria's eyes were dark, her cheeks flushed with desire. I traced her jawline with my thumb, my gaze never leaving hers.

"Maria," I whispered, my voice hoarse with need. "Say stop if you need to," I murmured.

She shook her head, her lips curving into a sly smile. "I won't," she replied, her voice a husky whisper.

I smiled, a slow, predatory grin that felt both foreign and exhilarating. "Good," I said, my voice thick with promise.

I stood, pulling her to her feet, our bodies still pressed together. The fire cast a warm glow over the room, illuminating the desire that burned in both of us. I backed her toward the wall, my hands roaming over her body, mapping the curves and contours I'd only imagined until now. Maria's hands clutched at my shirt, her nails digging into my skin as she pulled me closer.

"Luke," she murmured, her voice a plea and a promise all at once. I kissed her again, my lips moving to her neck, her collarbone, savoring the taste of her skin. Maria tilted her head back, her breath coming in short gasps as my mouth trailed lower, my hands moving to the hem of her shirt.

She lifted her arms, allowing me to pull the fabric over her head. Her bra followed, revealing breasts that were full and perky, her nipples tight buds of desire. I groaned, my mouth watering at the sight, and leaned in, taking one into my mouth, my tongue swirling and teasing until she moaned, her hands tangling in my hair.

"You're killing me, Luke," she gasped, her voice thick with need. I smiled against her skin, my hands moving to the button of her jeans.

"Not yet," I murmured, my voice a low rumble. "But soon."

I worked the button free, my fingers brushing her skin as I slid the zipper down. Maria's breath hitched, her body trembling with anticipation. I pushed her jeans and panties down her legs, baring her to my gaze. Her scent was musky and intoxicating. I groaned, my groin throbbing with need, and dropped to my knees, my mouth hovering inches from her core.

"Luke," she whispered, her voice a plea.

I looked up, meeting her gaze, and smiled. "Trust me," I said, my voice firm.

Maria nodded, her hands gripping my shoulders as I leaned in, my tongue dipping into her wetness. She tasted like heaven, her essence sweet and addictive. I moaned, the sound vibrating against her sensitive flesh, as I lapped at her, my tongue flicking and teasing, exploring every inch of her. Maria cried out, her body arching off the wall, her hips bucking against my mouth.

"Oh God, Luke," she panted, her voice hoarse with pleasure. "Don't stop."

I didn't. I feasted on her, my mouth and tongue working in tandem, driving her higher and higher. Maria's hands tangled in my hair, her nails scraping my scalp as she held me to her. Her moans filled the cabin, a symphony of pleasure that fueled my own desire. I could feel her building, her body tightening like a coiled spring, and I quickened my pace, my tongue flicking with relentless precision.

"Luke, I'm—" she gasped, her voice cutting off on a cry as her body shook with her release.

I held her through it, my mouth never leaving her, drinking in her essence as she came apart in my arms. Her cries echoed in the small space, a testament to the intensity of her orgasm.

When she finally stilled, her body slack against the wall, I stood, my hands gently lifting her. Maria's eyes were half-lidded, her expression dazed with pleasure. I smiled, a triumphant grin that felt both foreign and exhilarating.

"Your turn," she murmured, her voice a husky whisper.

I laughed, a low, rumbling sound that seemed to echo in the cabin. "You're insatiable," I teased, my hands moving to the button of my jeans.

Maria smirked, her confidence returning as she stepped closer, her hands brushing my chest. "And you're just getting started," she replied, her voice laced with promise.

I kicked off my jeans. I was thick and hard with need. Maria's eyes widened, her gaze raking over me with unabashed desire. "Impressive," she remarked, her voice dry. I smirked, unable to resist the urge to preen under her appraisal.

"If you want a job done, you call a Marine," I retorted, my voice dripping with sarcasm.

Maria laughed, a low, throaty sound that sent a jolt of desire through me. She stepped closer, her hands moving to my chest, her touch sending shivers down my spine.

"Prove it," she challenged, her voice a husky whisper.

I didn't need to be told twice. I pulled her against me, our bodies pressing together, my body nestled between her thighs. Maria moaned, her hands tangling in my hair as she kissed me fiercely, her tongue dueling with mine.

I groaned, the sound muffled against her lips, as my hands moved to her ass, lifting her onto me.

She gasped as I entered her, her body tight and wet, a perfect fit. I thrust upward, seating myself fully within her, our bodies moving in a rhythm as old as time. Maria cried out, her nails digging into my shoulders as she wrapped her legs around my waist, holding me to her.

I carried her to the couch, laying her down gently before hovering over her. The fire cast a warm glow over her body, illuminating the desire that burned in both of us. I thrust into her, our bodies moving in unison, the friction between us generating heat that rivaled the fire's warmth.

Maria met each thrust with one of her own, her body arching off the couch, her cries filling the cabin. I watched her, mesmerized by the sight of her pleasure, my own desire building to a fever pitch. Her hands moved to my back, her nails scraping my skin as she held me to her, her body tightening around me like a vice.

"Luke," she panted, her voice a plea. "I'm close."

I grinned. "Me too," I replied, my voice hoarse with need. I quickened my pace, our bodies moving faster, harder, the tension building until it was almost unbearable.

And then, with a cry that seemed to tear from her throat, Maria shattered, her body convulsing around me as she came. Her release triggered my own, pulsing deep within her as I spilled into her, my cries mingling with hers.

We lay tangled together, our bodies glistening with sweat, the fire crackling softly in the background. Maria's head rested on my chest, her breath coming in short gasps as her heart slowly returned to its normal rhythm. I stroked her hair, my fingers tangling in the strands, a sense of peace settling over me.

I looked down at Maria, her eyes closed, a soft smile playing on her lips. In that moment, I felt something I hadn't felt in a long time, hope. The future was uncertain, the fight unrelenting, but in this moment, with Maria in my arms, I felt invincible. I leaned down, pressing a gentle kiss to her forehead, my heart swelling with emotions I couldn't quite name.

I held her close, my mind adrift on a sea of possibilities. Would we make it out of this cabin, back to the world beyond? I didn't know. But as Maria's breath evened out, her body relaxing against mine, I realized it didn't matter. In this moment, with her in my arms, I was exactly where I was meant to be. And as the fire's glow cast long shadows on the walls, I closed my eyes, a sense of peace settling over me. Whatever the future held, we would face it together. For now, in the quiet of the cabin, I was content.

The world could wait. For now, there was only Maria and the warmth of the fire.

She brushed my hair back, eyes searching mine. "I've never done that before."

I lifted a brow in disbelief. "What, had sex?"

"No," she laughed quietly. "Given in. Like that. Let someone in without trying to control it."

I pulled her against me, folding her tight into my arms. Her head rested on my chest, and my heartbeat was loud enough for both of us.

"I've never let myself care this fast," I admitted. "It's dangerous."

"Everything is dangerous now."

Her voice was so small, I almost missed it.

"I'm scared," she whispered.

I kissed the top of her head. "I'll protect you."

"Not of the cartel. Of losing you."

I tightened my hold, mouth against her temple.

"Not happening," I whispered. "You hear me? I don't do one-night stands. I'm not going anywhere."

She sighed, and for the first time tonight, it was peaceful. Outside, the wind picked up. The cabin creaked, but I didn't move. She was asleep now, curled into me like it was the only place she had ever felt safe. I watched the shadows on the walls and counted each breath she took. I had done this before. Held someone in the quiet, pretended the world wouldn't take them away. But this felt different. Heavier. More real.

I had to dress. My gun stayed within arm's reach. I didn't close my eyes. I wouldn't risk it. Not with her lying here, trusting me with all the broken parts of herself. When the fire dimmed, I threw on another log. And then I saw it.

Tracks. Just outside the window. Fresh. Deep. Spaced wide like someone running. Not the man I neutralized earlier. Someone else. A scout. Maybe more. I stared at the prints and felt the sharp, familiar grip of tension flood my system. They knew where we were. And they were not backing off. I stepped around Maria carefully and grabbed my boots. She stirred but didn't waken.

Outside, the air was crisp and filled with pine. The prints stretched in both directions, coming from the east, curving toward the back of the cabin. I crouched low, fingers grazing the indentations. There were at least three sets. Three men. Close. Close enough to watch us without being seen.

I circled around to where I left the first guy, but he was still out cold. That ruled him out. These prints were fresh. Fifteen minutes, max. I headed back inside and locked the door behind me. Reinforced it with the wooden chair and slid the rifle closer.

Maria shifted, eyes blinking open. "What is it?"

"Tracks," I said. "Three sets. They were close."

She sat up fast, blanket slipping to her waist. "Are we safe?"

"Not yet."

I checked the bullets in the rifle and crouched beside the window.

"Get some sleep while you can," I said.

She didn't. Neither did I. We sat in the quiet for hours. The fire crackled low. Outside, the wind died down and fog began to creep across the forest floor. Maria didn't speak. But her hand slipped into mine and stayed there. Every few minutes, I checked the window. No movement. No voices. No lights. But I felt it in my gut. They were nearby. Watching. Planning.

Maria finally said, "What if we don't make it out of this?"

I glanced down at her. "We will."

"You can't promise that."

"No, but I can promise I'll die trying."

She gave me a crooked smile. "You're not exactly romantic."

"I'm trying to be honest."

"That's scarier."

I wrapped my arm around her shoulders and pulled her close. "We're not dying here. Not tonight."

The fire flared, just enough to warm her face. I kissed her temple and stayed ready, heart wired tight. We were not safe. But we were together. Somewhere between exhaustion and adrenaline, I rested my head against the wall and let my eyes close. Only for a minute. But the sound woke me instantly.

A twig snapped. Sharp. Deliberate.

I lifted the rifle and scanned the window. Nothing but trees and fog.

Maria sat up, wide-eyed. "What is it?"

"Someone's out there. Again."

I edged to the door and listened. Faint whispers. Maybe two voices. Spanish. Quick. Tense. I held up two fingers. She nodded. Another voice joined in. Then another.

Three. I grabbed the binoculars and lifted them just above the windowsill. Shapes moved in the gray mist. Shadows with weapons. Looking for the weak spot in our defenses. Maria crouched beside me, voice barely audible.

"We wait?"

I nodded. "Until they make a mistake."

And they would. Because they were here to hunt. But I knew terrain better than they did. I had SERE wilderness training. To become a Marine you had to qualify as a marksman with a rifle. And they didn't know I was ready to kill.

The mist faded with the coming light. Dawn broke slow and cold. The fire had died to embers, and Maria was dozing with her head on my shoulder again. I didn't move. I just watched the tree line. And then I saw them.

Footprints. Dozens. Crossing and crisscrossing outside the cabin. Some old. Some fresh. A full sweep. Circling like wolves. I eased out from under her and stepped outside, rifle ready. No movement now, but the message was clear. They knew where we were. They'd been testing our defenses. Seeing if we shot blind. Waiting for the right moment.

I crouched beside the doorframe and traced the prints with my hand. Big boots. Tactical spacing. At least six. Maybe more. They didn't attack last night because they weren't ready. But soon, they would be. I stepped back inside and locked the door. Maria stirred, blinking at me.

"What is it?"

I met her eyes. "They're coming."

Storm on the Mountain

Maria Sinclair

I woke to silence that wasn't right. Luke was already up, crouched by the window, rifle in hand. His body was tense, every muscle coiled. I followed his line of sight and saw the prints. Fresh ones. All around the cabin.

"They surrounded us overnight," he said quietly. "Six, maybe more."

My heart stuttered. There was no smoke, no gunfire, just that waiting stillness. Like the moment before a storm tore loose from the sky.

"What do we do?" I whispered.

Luke didn't look away. "We hold them off."

That was it. No panic, no drama. Just pure steel in his voice. I crawled toward the duffel bag and started pulling out supplies. Not weapons, anything I could use to paint with, markers, paper, tape, glue. Not usually tools for war, but I'd make them work.

"You're ... painting?" he asked.

"I'm rigging decoys. You said they might test the perimeter. Let's give them something to shoot at, to waste ammunition."

Luke gave me a look I could only describe as proud.

"Smart," he said.

I worked fast, layering overalls and jackets on broom handles and shaping silhouettes with blankets and duct tape. I painted rough faces on cardboard, shadows where eyes might be, bodies hunched like snipers in the trees. Luke snuck them outside in the brush, adjusting the angles with a sniper's eye.

"Movement triggers instinct," he said. "We'll make them jumpy."

Back inside, he started sealing windows with furniture, tipping over a table to brace the rickety door. I helped where I could, dragging a shelf across the front entry.

"Do you really think they'll wait to attack?" I asked.

"Cartel tactics change depending on who's leading but they like psychological games. They're waiting for us to make the first mistake."

A cold wind sneaked through the boards. My fingers stung with paint and cold. Then, a distant shot. I ducked instinctively. Luke didn't flinch. He glanced through the rifle scope and nodded.

"They took the bait."

Outside, a painted decoy crumpled.

We got their attention. Now we just had to survive it. The first real assault came fast. Glass shattered on the back window. Luke returned fire instantly, aiming low and wide. I stayed behind the couch, heart pounding so hard I felt it in my teeth. Then silence.

"Two down," he said.

I peeked over the edge. Snow had started. Light at first. A whisper of flurries against the trees. But it was building. I'm not sure whose side it favored.

"They'll use the storm," Luke muttered. "Noise cover, limited visibility. They think it gives them an edge."

"Does it?"

"Only if I let it."

I crawled over to him, ducking under the window. "How can I help?"

He blinked like he wasn't expecting the question. Then he pointed toward the bedroom.

"Nail boards under and over the windows. Use the hammer and those roofing nails from the closet."

I nodded and ran in a crouch. For the next hour, the only sounds were hammering, distant gunfire, and wind picking up speed. Snow turned everything white. Erased the world. But not the fear. That only grew sharper. The temperature dropped fast. My fingers went numb. Every nail I hammered felt like a risk, too much noise, not enough strength. But I did it anyway.

Luke moved like a machine. Calm. Exact. Every motion designed for defense. He turned the living room into a kill zone, cleared lines of sight, choke points, fallback positions. It was terrifying and brilliant.

Another shot cracked through the trees. This one hit the cabin wall, spraying splinters across the kitchen.

"They're testing our range," he said.

"And we're testing their patience," I replied not really understanding the range business.

He grinned without humor. "You're getting good at this."

I didn't feel brave. I felt tired and raw. But something in me had changed. I was not just a target anymore. I was in this fight. I figured I might as well be. Otherwise, I was just a sitting duck waiting for a bullet.

Then I heard something strange. A muffled crunch. Closer than before. I glanced out the side window and saw it. A shape. Pale coat. Rifle. Too close.

"Luke," I whispered. "They're coming in from the south."

His face hardened as he swiveled.

"Then we finish him."

The snowstorm slammed into us just after noon. Thick flakes blew nearly sideways, and the sky turned the color of ash. Visibility dropped to almost nothing.

Luke moved faster, checking defenses. I heard his voice through the howling wind.

"Storm's worse than I thought. They won't stand back now. They'll come in close."

"Is that better or worse?"

"Depends on how much ammo we have left."

We didn't have enough. He gave me a short-barreled revolver and showed me how to hold it properly.

"Only if they breach," he said.

I nodded as my stomach dropped lower than the floor at the idea, clutching the cold steel. The wind knocked branches against the roof. Every sound was a possible enemy. Every silence was worse.

Then it happened.

The wall near the back door shuddered. A shoulder hit it. Hard.

Luke was there in an instant, firing through the gap in the boards.

Screams. A man fell. Another crashed against the side window. We were officially under siege. And I was terrified. But I didn't freeze.

I stood and took aim. One of them got through.

He kicked in the back door and lunged inside. I fired once, wide, the shot deafening in my ears. Luke spun and fired twice. The man dropped inches from me.

I stared at the body. At the gun still in his hand. My own arms were shaking. Luke touched my shoulder.

"You okay?"

I nodded. "No. But I will be."

He squeezed my arm once. We drew the body out of the way, reinforced the door again. More bullets slammed into the front of the cabin. Shattered glass, busted planks.

Luke returned fire, fast and controlled. His focus never wavered.

"You're amazing," I said before I could stop myself.

His mouth twitched. "Tell me that after we make it through the night."

A bullet punched through the window and grazed the wall beside me. I dropped instinctively. Luke pulled me flat down and covered me with his body.

"Stay low," he growled.

The storm howled.

But we were still fighting. Still alive. Time blurred. I didn't know how many hours passed. The storm got louder. The gunfire faded, then returned. Luke reloaded again and again. We were running out.

"If they push hard, we're done." he said.

I reached for his hand and squeezed. "Then we push harder."

He kissed me, fast and rough, and then he was up again, firing into the white blur outside. It happened fast. A shadow moved to the left. Luke turned, fired. Another to the right. Then another broke through the side wall. Luke spun to cover me. And the shot rang out. His body jerked. I screamed as he fell.

Blood stained his shirt. His hand clutched his side. I crawled to him, dragging him behind the overturned table.

"Luke!" My voice was raw.

"I'm okay," he said. But his face was gray.

"You're bleeding."

He nodded. "Keep them back."

I lifted the revolver with trembling hands. This time, I would not miss. I fired once. Twice. Hit one. Missed the other. The last man turned and ran into the storm. Then silence.

Real silence.

I sat there with Luke's blood on my hands, heart pounding, chest tight. He gritted his teeth and pushed himself into a sitting position.

"I need pressure on the wound," he gasped.

I grabbed a towel from the kitchen and pressed it against his side. He groaned, eyes closing for a second.

"I've got you," I whispered. "You're not dying on me."

He chuckled weakly. "Not planning on it."

I bandaged him as best I could, using every scrap of cloth I could find. Then I drew him closer to the fire and piled every blanket I could find on top of him. He watched me, barely awake.

"You saved me," he said.

I shook my head. "You saved me first."

Snow and sleet pounded against the roof. We're trapped. Alone. Bleeding. But alive. For now. The storm raged through the night.

I sat beside Luke, changing his bandage every few hours. His fever spiked and faded, but he stayed conscious. Barely. Outside, the wind shrieked like it wanted in. But the walls held. At dawn, I rose and stepped toward the window.

The world was white. Pure, untouched snow blanketed everything. But in that blankness, I saw the tracks. Dozens of them. Crisscrossing the clearing. Circling the cabin like sharks around a sinking ship. They had retreated. For now. But they would come back.

I knelt beside Luke. His skin was clammy. Pale.

"We need help," I whispered. "Soon."

He opened one eye, barely awake. "Radio?"

"Dead. Frozen over."

He gritted his teeth and tried to sit. "Then we dig out. First light. South trail." His voice faded again.

I tucked the blanket tighter around him, shaking my head. Like he would be walking anywhere. We would fight again. But for now, we waited. Outside, the prints reminded me. The cartel wasn't done. But neither were we.

Breathless

Luke Turner

P ain brought me back.

Not the sharp kind. The dull, smothering kind that made it hard to think. I tried to sit up and immediately regretted it.

"Don't move," Maria whispered, crouched beside me. Her hands were firm on my chest, but they were shaking. So was her voice.

"I need to... repack it," I muttered.

"Tell me what to do."

She was already tearing the bandage off. Blood seeped out, dark and slow.

"Clean it first. Rubbing alcohol if we have it. Pressure. Tape."

She nodded, bolted for the supply bag. Every second dragged. I faded, the ceiling going gray around the edges. When she returned, her face was pale, determined.

"This is going to hurt," she warned.

I almost laughed.

She poured the alcohol over the wound. Fire erupted across my side. I grunted, biting down on the inside of my cheek.

"You're okay," she said, repeating it like a prayer. "You're okay. Stay with me."

I tried. But everything tilted sideways. I woke again to her voice.

"Luke. You have to drink."

She was holding a bottle to my lips. I managed a swallow of icy water. It burned on the way down. My body felt like it was wrapped in lead. I couldn't move much. I didn't want to. Some bodyguard. But her face was close, and her eyes were locked on mine.

"I think the bullet grazed your kidney," she said. "I stopped the bleeding for now, but if it starts again..."

"Doesn't matter," I rasped. "Get out. Take the trail."

She shook her head, furious. "No. I'm not leaving you."

"You have to."

"No. You protected me. Now I protect you."

Her voice broke on the last word. I tried to lift a hand, and she grabbed it. Held it tight like it was the only thing anchoring her. Then she kissed my knuckles. And stood. I heard the click of a chamber being loaded. The revolver.

"I'll handle it," she whispered fiercely.

And I believed her. I heard the creak of floorboards as she moved across the cabin. She didn't panic. Didn't rush. She was deliberate, checking the barricades, loading spare bullets into her pockets, double-checking the window slats. She was not a soldier. But she was brave. She knelt beside me once more and tucked the blanket tighter around my chest. Her fingers hovered at my jaw.

"I'll keep you safe," she whispered.

The words felt like a promise and a vow. Then she crossed to the front door and wedged a chair under the handle. She slid the table in place behind it. It was crude, but effective. Footsteps crunched in the snow outside. More than one. She froze. Her breath caught.

I forced my voice out. "South side. One blind spot behind the firewood."

She nodded and moved silently in that direction, revolver raised. I can't follow. I could barely see her now. The cold was pressing in again. I blinked. And she was gone.

Out of sight. Out there. Facing the nightmare alone.

The sounds were different now. Boots. Voices in low Spanish. Orders being given. They were closer than ever. I tried to move again and nearly blacked out. My side was burning. Wet. I knew what that meant.

Maria crouched beside the window, peeking through a crack. She held the revolver with both hands. Her breathing was sharp, but steady. She didn't know I could see her. She was shaking. But she stayed still.

One of them stepped into view. Tall. Bald. Heavy black coat and a rifle slung low.

He scanned the tree line, then lifted his hand. Maria moved. She didn't hesitate. She fired, once. Missed. The man spun and dove for cover. More voices shouted. A burst of return fire shattered a corner of the window. She crawled toward the fireplace, reloaded, and positioned herself behind a stack of firewood like I taught her.

She's scared. But she's fighting. I tried to call her name, but my throat was raw. All I could do was lie there and hope. The front door groaned. Boots stomped onto the porch. Maria shifted her position again, pistol up, two-handed grip. She breathed slow through her nose. I recognized the voice that follows. Low. Cruel. Confident.

"Maria. Don't do anything stupid. Come out. We only want to talk."

Her face went pale. She knew that voice, too. I remembered the files. The photo pinned in the Sierra Bravo war room. Diego Ramos. Her uncle's old partner. The one who turned on him.

"I know you're in there," he said. "Your uncle didn't listen either. Look where that got him."

Her jaw tightened. I could see it from here.

"I don't want to harm you, girl. But if you make me... I'll make it hurt."

She didn't move. She didn't speak. I wanted to tell her to run. To hide. To survive. But I couldn't speak loud enough. She rose from her cover. Stood tall. Face to face with the devil from her family's past.

"Put the gun down, Maria," Diego called.

She didn't. He stepped into view. I saw him clearly now through the half-broken window. Scarred cheek. Designer jacket. Cold eyes.

"I was there when you were born," he said. "Held you before your mother did."

Maria lifted her chin. "Then you should have known better."

He chuckled. "Your uncle didn't tell you everything."

She stepped forward. "He told me enough. He told me you sold out your friends. Got rich off blood."

"I gave your family a future."

"No. You gave us a target."

He raised his rifle. "Last chance."

She didn't flinch.

"Put it down," he said.

"I don't think so."

She fired first. Hit the post beside him. Missed his chest by an inch. The porch exploded into motion. Shouts. More gunfire. I tried to move. Get up. Help. But my legs won't work. Maria ducked behind the doorframe. She was shaking. But she was not broken. She was not running.

I faded in and out. The sounds were muffled now. Gunfire like it was underwater. My chest rose and fell with effort. The bandage was soaked through again. But I heard her. Her voice cutting through it all.

"Come any closer and I will shoot you in the face."

It was Maria. Strong. Fierce. Terrified. But standing her ground. A crash shook the back wall. Someone was trying to breach again. I heard her boots scrambling on the floor, then another shot. A body dropped. She was fighting.

Every instinct screamed at me to get up and protect her. But I couldn't. Not yet.

I gritted my teeth and dragged myself a few inches closer to the duffel. Bullets cracked through the side window again. One hit the lamp. Sparks flew. Maria dove to cover me with her own body, shielding my head. She was panting. I wanted to tell her she's doing everything right.

But the world tilted again. Darkness pulled me under.

I woke to firelight. Maria was crouched beside me again, pressing gauze to my side. Her hands were stained red. Her cheeks were wet with tears she hadn't noticed.

"You came back," she breathed.

I nodded once. "Barely."

Outside, silence hung heavy. The last shots must have scared them off. Or maybe they were regrouping.

"We have to finish this," she said.

Her voice had changed. It was steadier. Sharper.

"You sure you're ready?" I whispered.

She nodded. She pressed a pistol into my hand. Not the revolver. One from a cartel fallen.

"Two clips. That's it."

"Then we make them count."

She helped me sit up. Every inch hurt, but I could move. A little. We watched the window together. I had no idea how many were left out there. There was nothing yet. But I could feel it coming.

"They'll send him again," she said. "Diego."

"Then we put him down."

She nodded once. Her jaw was set. She was not afraid of him anymore. And I didn't think she ever would be again.

Footsteps crunched outside. We both froze. Maria lifted the rifle. I pulled myself upright against the wall. A figure stepped into view.

It's him. Diego. Alone this time. Arms raised slightly. No rifle in hand.

"I want to talk," he said. "Truce."

Maria didn't lower her weapon. "Talk is cheap."

"I warned your uncle. Told him to take the deal."

"You killed him."

"I survived," he said. "Same thing."

I saw her grip tighten. She stepped onto the porch. I wanted to scream for her to stop, to come back inside. But I didn't. She held her ground.

"You made me a target," she said. "Now I'm making you one."

He smiled. "You won't shoot me."

Her hand didn't shake. "I already did." She pulled the trigger. *Click.* Empty.

He laughed once. Then a second click.

The backup pistol. Maria didn't miss. He dropped to his knees.

Behind her, more movement in the trees.

The storm wasn't over.

It was just beginning.

Reckoning

Maria Sinclair

S moke curled from the pistol in my hand. Diego was down, clutching his shoulder, snarling through clenched teeth. I didn't move. Not yet. My arm shook, but I kept the barrel steady.

"Next time, it won't be your shoulder."

Behind me, I heard Luke groan. I wanted to go to him. Every part of me did. But I couldn't afford to take my eyes off Diego.

He laughed. "You don't have it in you."

I stepped closer. "You sure about that?"

The men in the trees hadn't moved yet. They were waiting. Watching. I couldn't tell if they were scared of me or stunned by what just happened. Either way, I needed to use it.

"Back off," I called out, raising my voice. "Or I put the next one through his skull."

Silence. Then footsteps crunching but no one appeared. They were hesitating. Good. Because that was all I needed. Time. Just a few more minutes. Behind me, Luke let out a broken whisper.

"Dani? Sam?"

I turned fast, heart lurching.

Luke was pale, sweat soaking his shirt, his head rolling against the wall. His eyes weren't focused. They were looking through me.

"Dani," he said again, voice thin and broken. "Don't take the car. Not with her."

I knelt beside him, gently brushing the hair from his forehead. "Luke, it's Maria. I'm here. You're safe."

But he didn't hear me.

His eyes fluttered. "She wanted to paint. Said Sam was making me a birthday card. With glitter."

A jagged piece of my heart tore loose as I realized what he was seeing. His wife and son. The ones he lost.

"I told her I'd be back by noon," he whispered. "I should have driven faster." His whole body trembled. "I never got to tell her I was proud. Never told Dani she saved me."

My throat ached, but I swallowed it down. "You have to stay with me now, Luke. You still have someone to fight for."

I squeezed his hand. "Me."

Luke blinked slowly, lips parting like he was trying to form words. I leaned in, clutching his hand tighter, willing him to come back to me.

Then, barely audible, "Maria..."

Relief flooded my chest. "Yeah. I'm here."

His gaze found mine, bleary but present. For a second, we were both silent.

Outside, the wind shifted. I heard branches creak. A crunch of snow. The cartel wasn't gone. They were regrouping. I stood and picked up the gun. My fingers curled around the grip like I was born to hold it.

"You stay here," I whispered. "Breathe. That's your only mission now."

Luke's lips twitched like he wanted to argue, but he nodded.

I moved back to the broken doorway. Diego was gone. Blood on the snow, but no body. I scanned the trees. Shadows shifted. Nothing solid. Nothing clear.

"You had your chance," I shouted. "Back off."

More silence. Then, a voice I didn't recognize.

"You're just a girl."

I smiled without humor. "And you're just a corpse who hasn't fallen yet."

I scanned the slope, trying to count how many voices I heard earlier. At least three remained. Maybe more. One stepped into view. Hooded. Tactical gear. AR slung low. He was bold, thinking I wouldn't shoot. I raised the gun, two-handed. My stance felt solid now. Not perfect, but grounded.

"Put it down," he said.

"You first."

He chuckled. "You think you're a hero?"

"No," I said. "I think I'm alive. And I plan to stay that way."

I squeezed the trigger.

Snow exploded beside him. Let him think it's a warning shot. He flinched, then scrambled for cover. More shouting followed. I ducked behind the frame and breathed through the surge of adrenaline. My pulse was everywhere. My skin felt too tight. But I was still standing.

Luke groaned again. I crawled back to him, cradling his head against my lap.

"I'm not leaving you," I whispered.

He opened one eye, dazed. "You're kind of amazing."

"Aw, tell me something I don't know."

Gunfire cracked from the trees. I grabbed the gun and pushed Luke deeper behind the couch. Plaster shattered. Splinters flew. I didn't hesitate. I returned fire, two controlled shots, just like Luke taught me. Then silence again. I crouched, chest heaving. My ears rang, but I listened hard. Boots crunched. Someone's trying to flank us.

I moved quickly, silent across the cabin, stepping around Luke. He watched me, eyes wide but clear.

"Right window," he rasped. "Wait three seconds."

I nodded and counted.

One one thousand. Two one thousand. Three.

A shadow shifted.

I fired.

A cry cut the air and something heavy crashed into the snow.

One down.

I ducked and counted my bullets, hands slick with sweat and paint from earlier. I didn't feel like a CEO's pampered daughter anymore. I didn't feel like a pawn. I felt like a damn warrior. At least a survivor.

"Keep breathing," I called to Luke. "I'm not finished yet."

Outside, another voice shouted, angry, desperate. This time, I recognized it.

"Maria!" Diego's voice cut through the snow and smoke. "You don't want to die for this. You're not built for this life."

I pressed my back to the wall and closed my eyes for half a second. Just one breath. Then I stepped into the doorway and raised my voice. "You don't get to define me anymore."

"You're scared."

"Yeah," I shouted. "And I'm still standing. You came for a weak little girl. But she's left the party."

The woods went quiet.

Luke's voice was barely a whisper. "That's it. Keep talking. Make them doubt."

So, I do.

"My uncle died protecting something. You? You've killed for money and power. But the people you command? They don't trust you. You're losing them."

I spotted a movement. One of the shadows hesitated. A muzzle lowered. Diego must have seen it too, because he fired toward the trees, not the cabin. His control was slipping. I was sure the cartel would gladly punish his failure. I pressed the advantage.

"Lay down your guns. Walk away, and I won't chase you."

Diego snarled. But no one shot. Not yet.

Snow swirled in the wind between us. My arms ached, but I didn't lower the gun.

"You really think this ends with you winning?" Diego called out, voice bitter. "Even if you kill me, there'll be more."

"I'm not looking to win," I shouted back. "Just to survive. And you? You already lost."

I didn't know if it was the words or the way I said them, but one of the men stepped into view with his rifle raised, above his head. He was surrendering or at least giving up the fight. A second man followed, hands out, eyes never meeting mine.

Diego screamed. "Cowards!"

He raised his own weapon and fired at the second man, dropping him.

I shot towards Diego. Not at Diego. Not yet. But close. A warning.

Luke groaned behind me. I heard him trying to get up, but his body wouldn't let him. I steadied myself and called out one more time.

"Anyone else want to die for this guy?"

Silence.

I lowered my aim and stepped forward. Diego stepped into view. We both fired. The gunshots echo through the trees. One shot. Then two. I stumbled back, breath caught in my throat. I was still standing. My shoulder burned, but I didn't feel anything wet. Not yet.

Diego hit the snow hard, face twisted in fury. His rifle skittered away. He was hit, chest or gut. I couldn't tell which. And I don't know if I hit him or it was one of his own guys.

Behind me, Luke was slumped against the wall, pistol in his lap, smoke trailing from the barrel. His eyes met mine.

"Did we get him?" he rasped.

I nodded, my body frozen.

Then Diego coughed. He was still alive, dragging himself toward the rifle, blood trailing behind him.

"No," I whispered.

I ran forward, kicking the rifle out of reach, and pressed my gun barrel to his chest. He grinned, teeth stained red. "You don't have the guts."

"I've got enough."

He laughed once, then sagged. Conscious? Unclear. I backed away, hands trembling. Behind me, Luke made a sound that was not a groan. It was worse.

I rushed to him. Blood pooled under his side. More than before.

"No," I whispered again. "No, no, no."

He tried to smile. "Told you I'd die trying."

"You're not dying. You're not allowed."

But his eyelids fluttered. Too fast. Too light. I pressed hard on the wound, shouting for him to stay with me. Outside, voices shouted. Footsteps ran. Some away. Some toward. I didn't know who was left. I didn't know what was coming.

All I knew was that Luke was fading.

And if he went, a piece of me went too. The best piece.

A shot cracked again.

I screamed.
I didn't know who fired.
I didn't know who fell.
The world tilted—
And everything went white.

Under Fire

Luke Turner

P ain anchored me to the floor, but adrenaline cut through it like a blade. I heard the crunch of snow. Boots. Close. I lifted the gun with both hands, elbows locked. My vision tunneled. There was a shadow by the porch, half-hidden behind the frame.

I fired.

The man jerked back, dropped. Not moving. Another behind him flinched, ran left. I pivoted, braced with my knee, and squeezed off two more rounds. One hit the doorframe. The second found his flesh. A howl split the air.

"Clear left," I rasped.

"Right side!" Maria's voice—sharp, solid, alive.

I crawled toward the couch for cover. My side burned like fire. Blood slicked my hip, but I didn't stop moving. Another shape rose through the window. I don't think. I shot. Glass shattered. A body hit the snow. Stillness.

Then—her hands on me. Warm, frantic.

"Luke—are you—"

"I'm here. Still here. Always." But barely.

Maria Sinclair

The cloud of white snow settled from the incoming helicopter blowing up its own snowstorm. Voices yelled. Radios crackled. I lifted the gun because I didn't know whether this was just more cartel coming in to finish the job. I was ready to protect Luke with my last breath.

Then one man stepped forward. I knew that stance. The squared shoulders. The way he entered like he owned the cabin. And there was a logo on his black tactical gear. In the center was a big SB, Sierra Bravo.

"Oh, god." I choked, nearly in tears.

"Who's the bodyguard in this sitch?" he asked, laughing.

"Help Luke." I cried.

"Yeah. Get a medic in here." He said into his radio, "I'm Tucker, Sierra Bravo, as if there's any doubt. You guys did such a good job of going dark we had to track Ortega radio's chatter to find you. We'll be hauling you back to a lovely secure bunker away from this mess though looks like my friend Luke may need to divert to a hospital, the showoff."

"There may be more of them out there." I said, standing back so a medic could get at Luke.

"Not anymore." Tucker said with a sharklike grin, "We like to tidy up our scenes before we leave. I'm guessing by the looks of this place you're going to be wanting a meal and a shower pronto. Ready for your extraction?"

"I'm not leaving Luke." I asserted.

Tucker

I looked at Maria as she lowered the gun. Eyes like her uncle's when he finally cracked. Luke was bleeding out behind her. I could see it in the pale blue under his fingernails. He was holding on by grit and bone.

"Stand down," I said to the agent at my flank.

He didn't move.

"Now."

He lowered his rifle.

I crouched next to Maria and Luke. "You still alive, Turner?"

"He's been hallucinating." Maria said, wiping away tears.

"Barely," Luke muttered.

"Good." I leaned in. "You're gonna want to stay that way. This storm's only half over."

Luke Turner

I hated that I needed his help. Tucker's voice was the same as it was the day we raided that weapons' cache outside Kandahar. Calm. Cold. Always three steps ahead. He saved my life back then. Then vanished when it counted. Now he was hauling me into a helicopter while Maria pressed her hands to my side, whispering things I can't hold on to.

"Tucker," I croaked. "If you screw her over..."

He didn't flinch. "I won't."

"You already did."

He shut the door.

The cabin disappeared below us. The storm thinned as we headed downhill. Maria sat next to me, arms wrapped tight around her middle like she was holding something broken inside. I wanted to hold her instead. But I couldn't even lift my hand.

Tucker handed her a flash drive. "Your uncle's full testimony. Accounting records. Wire transfers. Everything they killed to bury."

Maria didn't thank him. Neither did I. Trust had a cost. And we were still paying.

We made it to the safe house in a hour and a half. This one was a low-slung former government facility outside Durango. Snow-blasted, faceless. Cameras on every corner. Two agents in dark windbreakers met us at the gate. Maria didn't speak as they led us inside.

They put me on a gurney, ran IVs. The pain meds kicked in fast. Too fast. I hated the floating. Maria hovered at the edge of the curtain while a nurse checked my vitals.

"You're stable," she said softly. "But you lost a lot of blood."

"Will I fight again?" I managed.

She smiled. "Give it time."

I watched Maria pace the hallway. She'd changed. The defiance in her spine was still there, but there was a new edge too. A weight. A knowledge she didn't have before. Tucker emerged from a glass-walled conference room. His expression was unreadable. He said something to her. She froze, then nodded. Something was wrong. And I felt it in my bones before I even heard the words. Maria stepped through the curtain. Her face was pale. Her eyes, haunted.

"What did he say?" I asked, immediately.

She didn't answer right away. She just moved to the edge of my bed and sat, hands clenched in her lap.

"They found Mia." she whispered, tears leaking to slowly course down her cheeks.

"It's not on you." I said fiercely reaching for her hand. She didn't need to explain. The cartel didn't leave around witnesses.

"I know but ... I still feel it."

I just held her hand, tightly. I had nothing better to offer.

"What else?"

"They offered me something."

I waited.

"Witness protection."

The words were low. Meant to be stable. They landed like a sucker punch. I pushed myself up on one elbow. Pain flared. I didn't care.

"They want you to disappear?"

She nodded. "New name. New life. Gone by morning."

"They're serious?"

"Tucker said it's the only way to keep me alive. The cartel will regroup. They always do."

I nodded, swallowing.

Her lip trembled, just once. "There's no us in witness protection, Luke. I go, or I stay and die."

I reached for her hand. She let me hold it. She didn't say anything. Not when it might have broken us both.

Maria Sinclair

I have never felt so torn. Luke's hand was rough and warm in mine. His fingers twitched like he was holding back everything he wanted to say.

"I don't want to lose you," he said.

"You won't," I lied and we both knew it.

Because that was what this felt like, losing him. Losing me. Again. I turned away, staring at the sterile tiles on the wall. Witness protection wasn't just a relocation. It was a rebirth. A lie that lasted forever. I'd never paint again under my own name. I'd never touch the life I built before all this. And Luke? He wouldn't be there on the other side.

"I don't want to run," I whispered.

Tucker appeared at the door. "They need your answer within the hour. Helicopter's waiting."

I nodded, numb. Luke squeezed my hand tighter. One hour. To decide who I was. To decide who I left behind. To decide if love was worth dying for.

Luke Turner

I've faced death more times than I could count. But this? Watching Maria wrestle with this decision in silence? This was worse. She wouldn't look at me anymore. Like if she did, the dam would break.

"You have to go," I said again.

She pressed her palm to my chest. "And if I stay? How long before they find me again? How long before I have to watch you bleed in the snow a second time?"

I didn't have an answer. The worst part was, I got it. Every piece of logic screamed for her to run. But my heart? It was hanging by a thread.

"Do you love me?" I asked.

She didn't hesitate. "Yes."

"Then there's no choice. I can't watch you die."

Her voice trembled. "If I stay, you might die."

She turned away, biting her lip. The nurse brought in fresh clothes. One hour, they said. Now it felt like seconds.

Maria Sinclair

They gave me thirty minutes to pack. It was kind of a joke. I didn't have anything to pack. Thirty minutes to erase a lifetime. I stood in the guest room, staring at the folded sweatshirt they issued, the plain duffel bag, the fake driver's license tucked inside an envelope.

Name: Morgan Ellis. Age: 27. Occupation: Administrative Assistant.

Not artist. Not fighter. Not the woman who bled in the snow beside the man she loves.

I could hear Luke down the hall. He was arguing with Tucker, his voice low and rough. He still didn't trust him. Neither did I. But I was out of options. Then I looked in the mirror. Did I look like Morgan yet? I didn't even look like Maria. Certainly no party girl.

I closed the bag. My hand hovered over the zipper. Then I unzipped it again. And added the photo I drew of Luke's smile on the safehouse napkin. I might have to run.

But I can't forget.

Luke Sinclair

She walked into the infirmary with the duffel slung over one shoulder. No makeup. Hair pulled back. New clothes that didn't fit her body or her soul. Maria, remade as Morgan Ellis. She stood at the edge of my bed, eyes red, chin up.

"I have to go," she said.

I nodded. It was the only part of me I could move without wincing.

"You don't have to say anything," she added, her voice tight.

"I do."

She closed her eyes.

I tried to sit up straighter. "You saved my life. You didn't have to. You could've run back at the cabin. Could've left me to bleed out in the snow."

She swallowed. "You didn't leave me either."

"I couldn't."

"I can't stay."

I nodded again. But this time, my jaw clenched.

"You asked if love was worth dying for," I said.

She nodded slowly.

"It is. But it's also worth living for. And I think we earned that."

Her breath caught.

"Come with me," she whispered.

"You know I can't."

She knew. And that was the part that broke me.

A knock interrupted. Tucker leaned in. "Time's up."

Maria leaned down, kissed my forehead.

I closed my eyes to hold the feel of her lips there.

"Goodbye," she said.

I can't answer. Because if I did— I would never let her leave.

Goodbye Isn't Forever

Morgan Ellis (Maria Sinclair)

The antiseptic scent of the hospital was sharper than usual, like it was trying to scrub the memory of what happened out of the air. I sat beside Luke's bed, staring at the white bandages wrapped around his ribs, rising and falling with each breath. His face was pale beneath the bruises, but his eyes, God, those intense green eyes, are sharp, watching me like he was memorizing every inch of me.

"I hate this," I whispered, fingers laced tightly in my lap. "I hate everything about this."

Luke shifted with a grunt, the movement making him wince. "You're not the only one."

I forced a laugh, but it came out brittle. "You almost died."

"Didn't. You're not getting rid of me that easy."

I bit my lip, swallowing against the lump in my throat. "Tucker says the FBI has a clean window. They can move me out tonight. New name, new city. They think it's the safest option."

His jaw tightened. "It is."

"But it means leaving everything behind." I shook my head, my voice cracking. "You. My art. My life."

Luke pushed himself a little higher on the pillow, his hand reaching for mine. I gave it to him because I was weak, because I could not *not* touch him when I knew this might be the last time. His palm was warm, fingers rough and strong.

"I've watched people I care about get caught in the crossfire," he said, voice low and raw. "I can't do that again. I can't lose you, Maria."

"You're not losing me." I leaned in, forehead resting against his. "You're giving me a chance to live."

His breath shuddered. "Then take it."

The hours crawled like shadows across the hospital wall. Nurses came and went, checking vitals, adjusting machines, offering polite distractions I can't afford. I stayed curled up in the armchair beside Luke's bed, refusing to sleep, knowing every second that passed brings us closer to the part I've been dreading. The goodbye.

I stood, walking to the window to hide the way those words wrecked me. The city outside glowed under streetlamps and sirens, neon and shadow, noise and life. Somewhere out there, a whole new identity was waiting for me. A life with no Luke in it.

"They said I could still do art somewhere." I didn't turn around. "I'll get a cat. Maybe take up pottery."

His chuckle was dry. "Pottery sounds dangerous. You'd find a way to throw it at someone."

I finally looked back at him. "I don't want to go."

"I know."

"But I will. Because if I stay, they'll find me. And they'll use me to hurt you. Or kill you."

Luke didn't argue. That was how I knew how much this costed him. He lifted the dog tag chain from around his neck, fingers shaking, and held it out. "Take this. So, you don't forget."

I walked over, eyes blurring, and closed my fingers around it. "I couldn't forget you if I tried."

Tucker arrived just after midnight. He was wearing civilian clothes now, jeans, dark jacket, clean-shaven. He looked more like a guy picking up a date than an undercover agent. But his eyes were all business.

"You ready?" he asked, not unkindly.

No. "Yes," I lied.

Luke sat upright with effort, fighting through the pain. I hated how pale he looked. I hated that I was not going to be here when he woke up tomorrow. I hated that this was necessary.

Tucker stepped aside as a nurse wheeled in a chair. "We'll take you out through the service elevator. Car's waiting in the alley. No lights, no chatter. You'll have a burner in the glovebox until we hand you off."

"Will I get to call?" I asked. "Just once?"

Tucker hesitated. "Probably not."

Luke tried to stand, and I rushed to steady him. His arm looped around my shoulders, his body trembling with the effort. But he would not let go until I did.

"I don't get to ask you to stay," he said roughly. "But if I could, I'd ask."

Tears spilled before I could stop them. "And I'd say yes. Every time."

He kissed me. It was not frantic or desperate. It was slow and sure and final. Like he was branding every nerve with the memory of this moment, because it was the last we got. I sunk into it, burning it into my bones.

When we broke apart, Tucker gave me a nod. "Time."

Luke leaned against the wall, still on his feet, still watching. I turned one last time at the door. "You better be alive when I get back." The lie filled my eyes.

He gave me a crooked smile but his eyes were haunted with non-physical pain. "I'll be the guy with the limp and the scars. Try not to fall for anyone else."

The night swallowed me whole as we exited the hospital. I kept my head down, hood up, shoulders hunched like I was wearing someone else's skin. Because in a way, I was. Morgan Ellis, art teacher, cat owner, stranger to danger.

The SUV was dark and silent; its windows tinted against the world. I climbed into the back seat without a word. Tucker took the passenger side. A younger agent I didn't know drove, his expression blank. Nobody spoke. The silence was heavier than the hospital walls. Heavier than Luke's voice in my head telling me to go, to live, to survive. But I didn't want survival without him. I didn't want to be safe if it meant numb. Still, I let them drive me away from everything I had ever known, learned I wanted.

We were miles outside the city when Tucker finally turned toward me.

"You did the right thing," he said.

I stared out the window. "Doesn't feel like it."

"Feelings don't always get to weigh in. This buys you time. The cartel won't stop, not while your uncle's still cooperating. But we've burned every lead they had on you tonight. You've got a head start."

I nodded, not trusting myself to speak.

At a rest stop around dawn, Tucker gave me a small, beat-up phone and a new ID. He didn't say much, just handed over the items like he'd done it a hundred times. Maybe he had.

"You'll meet a contact at the bus station in Santa Fe. She'll get you set up."

Santa Fe. Mountains and isolation. A place to disappear. I should have felt relief. Instead, I felt hollow. But I took the phone. I took the ID. I took the bag with cash and a change of clothes. Because Luke asked me to. Because if I was not brave enough to stay, then I had to be brave enough to start over.

The sun was barely up when I stepped off the bus. Santa Fe was quiet in the early light, the high desert air brisk enough to sting. I pulled my coat tighter and glanced around the station, just a few scattered travelers and a sleepy-looking attendant. No one payed attention to me. Good. That was the point.

I sat on a bench outside, phone in hand, heart thudding like I had committed a crime just by existing. I didn't know what I expected, an escort, a welcome sign, maybe a kind face to make this feel less like exile. But there was no one. Until there was.

Risking It All

Luke Turner

T he maps never told me anything useful. Not really. Not when it came to her. I'd scoured every trail the Bureau left behind, pulled favors from half the ghosts in my black-ops past, and scrolled through months of encrypted data looking for just one thread that led to her. Maria had vanished the way the best fugitives do. Completely.

Until last week, when a bartender in New Mexico posted a photo of his café. In the blurry background was a mural of crashing waves painted across the side of the building. Vibrant. Wild. Familiar.

It was her art.

Now I stood on a cracked sidewalk in a quiet town so small it barely earned a dot on the map, staring at a café painted like the ocean itself had risen and taken root on desert adobe walls. The mural looked newer. Fresh strokes. She was alive. Here.

My hands clenched at my sides, as the screen door creaked open. And she stepped out.

She froze when she saw me. Her eyes went wide, mouth parted, paint-streaked brush still clutched in one hand. For a beat, neither of us moved. Then her lips trembled, and she dropped the brush.

"Luke?"

The sound of my name in her voice nearly undid me. I took a step forward, then another, until I was close enough to see the flecks of blue paint on her cheek. Her curls were longer. Her eyes looked older. But she was here. Real. Breathing. Alive.

"I found you," I said, voice thick.

Her hand rose slowly, as if she didn't trust it to hold steady. When her fingers touched my chest, right over my heart, I covered them with mine.

"You're not supposed to be here," she whispered.

"Couldn't stay away."

Her breath caught. "They'll come after you."

"Let them."

The air between us cracked with something volatile. Something waiting to be set *loose*. Her eyes searched mine like she didn't know whether to kiss me or slap me.

I solved the dilemma for her. I kissed her. She surged into me like a dam breaking, hands fisting in my shirt, mouth urgent and hungry. My back hit the café's outer wall, and I barely felt the impact. All I could feel was her, soft, warm, alive in my arms again.

I gripped her waist, lifted her easily, her legs wrapping around me without hesitation. The kiss deepened, wild and unrestrained. We didn't need words. The pain of separation, the hunger, the love that never left us, it all poured out in the way our mouths collided.

"I missed you," she breathed against my lips.

"Not as much as I missed you."

She laughed, half-broken. "I was going to call. I swear. But they told me—"

I silenced her with another kiss, slower this time, letting the ache bleed out between us. Her body molded to mine, and something settled in my chest. She was here. We had this.

"Where's your place?" I asked, voice low against her ear.

She pointed toward the side street. "Second floor. Green door."

I didn't let her walk. I carried her the whole way.

Her apartment was small but bright, windows open to the breeze, half-finished canvases leaning against the walls. Paint-stained rags were tossed over a battered armchair. It smelled like lemons and linseed oil, and something that was just her.

I kicked the door shut with my boot.

She kissed me again before I could speak, dragging me toward the couch with a heat I hadn't felt since the night in the cabin. Her hands tugged my shirt over my head, fingers tracing scars she remembered. When her mouth followed the path, I groaned.

"You kept the dog tag," I murmured, catching the chain glinting at her neck.

She nodded. "Never take it off."

I stripped her top, slow enough to savor the way her breath hitched. My palms skimmed over her curves, her warmth drawing a shiver down my spine. I kissed my way down her throat, past the salt-sticky edge of her collarbone, memorizing every sound she made.

When she pulled me on top of her, nothing else mattered. Not the cartel. Not the past. Only this. Only us. I took my time relearning her. Her body was familiar and new all at once, every gasp and moan like a prayer I hadn't realized I was still waiting to hear. She arched under me, nails digging into my back, guiding me with a hunger that matched my own.

Clothes disappeared. Skin met skin. She wrapped around me like she had never left, pulling me in deeper with every breathless plea. I braced myself above her, watching her face twist in pleasure as our bodies found that perfect rhythm. Her mouth parted, her eyes wide and wild.

"You feel like home," she whispered.

I kissed her, hard and slow, before answering. "You are my home."

Her hands tangled in my hair, dragging me closer as our movements became frantic. We were lost in each other, a storm of sweat and sound, mouths and hearts syncing until the world outside the walls no longer existed. When she shattered beneath me, I followed her over the edge with a growl torn from my chest.

We collapsed together, hearts racing. Her fingers traced circles over my shoulder, the silence filled only by our breath. For a long time, we didn't speak. I just held her, one hand tracing the length of her spine, the other buried in her hair. Her cheek rested against my chest, heartbeat slowing in sync with mine.

She tilted her face up, eyes heavy but clear. "You're staying?"

"If you'll have me."

"Only for the rest of your life."

The words wrapped around me like armor. All the doubt and guilt and time we'd lost, it dissolved in the space between her words and the way she looked at me.

"I broke protocol to find you," I said. "They might pull my license. Hell, I might go to jail."

Her smile was sleepy and full of fire. "Then I'll paint your mugshot."

I chuckled, brushing a strand of hair from her cheek. "You're trouble."

"You knew that already."

My hand found hers and laced our fingers. "I don't care about consequences. I just want a life with you. Not stolen moments. The real thing."

She leaned up and kissed me, soft this time. Like a promise.

"You've got it."

We spent the rest of the afternoon curled together on the couch, a tangled mess of limbs and whispered questions. She told me about her job at the café, the local gallery that sold her prints, the night terrors that hadn't gone away.

I told her about the fallout from our disappearance. Tucker covering for me. The FBI furious but quiet, not wanting to explain how one of their witnesses vanished and reappeared with a bodyguard in tow.

"They're not actively hunting us," I said. "But they're watching."

"So, we keep low," she said. "Play it smart."

"I can do smart."

Her fingers trailed over my chest. "I don't need hiding. I need a life."

"You want to go public?"

She hesitated, then nodded. "Eventually. When it's safe. But for now, I want to live without fear. I want to paint what I want. Love who I want."

I kissed her again, slow and deep, heart full of her. "Then we'll do it your way. On your terms."

She smiled. "As long as you're with me."

"Always."

She looked at me, her voice suddenly soft. "Can we finally start our real life?"

Art and Armor

Morgan Ellis (Maria Sinclair)

After our classes are over, we clean up the last of the wine glasses and stack chairs while the wind slips through the open door of our studio, Art & Armor. I pull down a painting from the front display to take home, and Luke finishes locking up the gym mats in the back. We move like a team now. Outside, the street is mostly empty. The neon sign buzzes faintly overhead, casting a soft blue glow on the sidewalk. We stand in the doorway, watching the stars blink overhead.

"You ever think we'd end up here?" I ask.

He looks out at the horizon, then back at me. "Honestly? No. But I hoped."

I take a deep breath, and the words bubble up before I can stop them. "I want more."

Luke stills.

"Not just this," I continue. "Not just the studio or the paintings or the peace."

He turns fully to me. "What do you want?"

I step closer, placing my hands on his chest.

"I want to make our own family. Whatever that looks like. You and me. Something that's just ours."

Luke blinks, then his face softens. A slow grin spreads across his lips, the kind that makes me weak in the knees.

"You serious?" he asks, voice low.

"Dead serious," I say. "I don't care if it's kids or dogs or a cactus we name after your old commander. I just want a future that belongs to us."

He pulls me in close, wrapping his arms around me until I'm pressed to his chest, my cheek against the steady rhythm of his heart.

"Let's do it," he murmurs. "Let's make something new."

I laugh, giddy and breathless. "You're not freaking out?"

"I've faced down warlords and drug lords. I think I can handle a baby. Or a cactus."

I tilt my head up. "Always so confident."

He kisses me, soft and sure. "Only when it comes to you."

We walk hand in hand back toward our apartment above the studio. The door creaks, the wood floors groan under our feet, and everything feels exactly right.

As we disappear inside, I whisper into the night air, "Let's make our own family."

Luke answers with a grin. "Always."

Want to join Jax' Inner Circle?

E very Jax Kane book has a secret code word at the end.
Collect them to unlock sneak peeks, bonus chapters, and early cover reveals.

Your secret code word for *Locked Down with the Bodyguard* is:

SNOWBOUND.

Enter it here to start your collection:

https://forms.gle/JTGzCbssuofe3HTp8

A Few Final Words From Jax

H i, Jax Friend!

I hope you enjoyed reading *Locked Down with the Bodyguard* as much as I enjoyed writing it!

Did you know that reader reviews are largely what determine how books get ranked when someone searches on Amazon?

It is **vitally** important for indie creators, like me, to get reviews from people like you.

So, please consider heading over to Amazon and giving this book an honest sentence or two review. You can just look up the book: *Locked Down with the Bodyguard* by Jax Kane. OR click the link https://amzn.to/4nfNl9H

And if you liked this Sierra Bravo Security adventure, there are more for you to read!

Protecting the Grumpy CEO where a bodyguard has to persuade the CEO that her life is in danger and stop outsiders from stealing her world changing software!

Stuck with my Ex's Brother. A plane crash frees a killer and a bodyguard flees with a nurse into a blizzard hoping to contact the authorities. https://amzn.to/3JljfDY

Follow me on my Amazon author page to get 1st notice about my new releases! Another new Sierra Bravo Security story is coming soon about a pop star being stalked and her Sierra Bravo bodyguard! Here's the address www.amazon.com/author/jaxkane and an easy link https://www.amazon.com/author/jaxkane

And if you haven't read the first book in the Sierra Bravo Security series, *Pretending with the Protector*, you can get it here for **FREE** https://dl.bookfunnel.com/ono7q131mr

Thanks for reading! Readers mean everything to me.

Your friend,

Jax

www.ingramcontent.com/pod-product-compliance
Lightning Source LLC
Chambersburg PA
CBHW050456110726
47899CB00003B/960